WHITE TALONS

The Complete

BLACK MASK

Cases of Tex of the Border Service

KATHERINE BROCKLEBANK

---

primary illustrator: Arthur Rodman Bowker

cover by Jes Schlaikjer

BLACK MASK

2023

Table of Contents

Bracelets

A tale of Tia Juana after the closing hour of the Border and all the good folks have gone home

TEX WATCHED FROM THE CORNERS of her eyes, watched, with a tight little pucker around her heart.

The girl seemed so young, so incongruous in that blatantly obvious setting. She was like a flower from an old-fashioned garden and yet there she was in the ribald atmosphere of the *Blue Fox*—where Pancho, the shifty-eyed Mexican proprietor, rubbed his palms together and smiled his oily smile to his patrons; where Eddie swung his bamboo cane to the syncopated time of his moaning Hopa-Holi orchestra—Eddie who wore a chocolate brown suit to match his complexion, a screaming orange tie and a straw hat, who sang the latest popular ballads in a voice—untrained, crooning—as insidious as the ether-doped drinks that the silken-voiced bartenders slid across the bars of Old Town, that were now world-famous, polished to a dull red glow by the elbows of many nationalities.

Tex shifted her eyes to the long mirror back of the bar, noting her titian wig with an inward smile of satisfaction. Strangely enough her greenish gold eyes took on a copper glint. Her wide, good-humored mouth had turned to one of hard wisdom under the clever manipulation of a vivid lipstick. The orange rouge, slapped carelessly on either cheekbone, gave the finishing touch to a Border percentage girl, calloused, eager—pathetic.

She eased away from the obese gentleman from Kansas City, who pawed her with maudlin intensity, and edged a little nearer to the girl. Her eyes traveled slowly over her, cognizant of the soft green silk dress; the skirt a bit longer than was smart, the floppy affair of black straw that shadowed her face. She seemed like a slender flower-stalk as she leaned against the bar, her arms draped across its stained surface, her fingers playing nervously with the string of bracelets she wore on her left wrist.

Tex noticed particularly the girl's hands. Narrow and white with long, thin fingers that were never still—fingers that hovered constantly over the bracelets—bracelets that caught and held Tex's attention. There were eight of them, Chinese, of intricate design, amber and gold, carved ivory, jade. They made a peculiar clanking sound whenever the girl moved her arm.

Tex let her gaze rove blearily along the string of heterogeneity that lined the bar: percentage girls, cheap, faded creatures with gold-filled teeth who wheedled unwilling male sightseers into buying them drinks; thrill-hunters; society matrons with a veneer of hauteur washed off by Border hooch; flappers; groggy daddies whose wives were abroad for the summer; doubtful ladies in shoddy evening clothes; crafty-eyed Mexicans; derelicts; law-dodgers.

Slowly Tex's eyes came back to the girl and the vain little fish-faced man who stood beside her. They had come in together and Tex knew from things she had heard—never mind how or where—that this must be "The Eel." A clever crook was The Eel, who had so far eluded the police, who was always under suspicion but had never been caught with the goods. He claimed to be Mexican, although his intimates knew that he was half Chinese. Under an assumption of intoxication Tex studied him closely. With his oily, mud-colored skin, slick black hair and opaque slanting eyes he resembled his pseudonym, and Tex imagined she'd want to wash her hands after

touching him. He looked—slimy.

Tex lurched against the girl. " 'Lo," she gurgled in her slightly husky voice.

The girl looked up at her, startled. " 'Lo," she answered involuntarily, without smiling.

The Eel bent forward, giving Tex a sharp glance of mistrust, but when he saw her grinning at him vacantly he turned back to the girl and continued his low-toned conversation.

Tex edged a little nearer, endeavoring to hear his whispered words. He stopped short and Tex felt instinctively that he was regarding her with suspicion in the bar mirror. She hooked her arm in the girl's in a sudden burst of alcoholic familiarity and felt the girl grow rigid—with fear? Tex wondered. "Have thish one on me, dearie," said Tex.

The girl relaxed and smiled wanly. "Oh—thank you." She pushed her empty glass across the bar.

"M'boy fren'll buy fur the crowd—won' yuh, honey?" Tex swayed toward the inebriated obesity from Kansas City, but he was slumped over the bar, oblivious to the percentage girls' ever consuming thirst.

Tex shrugged. "Nev' mind, dearie, Ah's good sport. Ah'll buy—mahshelf." She opened her stringy bead bag a crack and peered blearily into its shabby depths.

"Aw, lay off, will yuh?" The Eel scowled darkly at her, flipped a coin to the bartender, grasped the girl by the arm, and pushed her through the crowd of black-bottom maniacs on the dance floor to the door.

Through the medium of the bar mirror Tex watched them vanish into the one main street, a street that was already growing dusk, a street that, after dark, was deserted, stealthy, dangerous—for those visitors who are foolish enough to loiter.

Tex loitered, loitered until the music stopped abruptly with harsh discordance; until the last stream of sightseers stampeded for the Border; until the gambling halls and open-fronted cantinas closed with mock modesty and a final sly wink of lights; until night shrouded the wicked little town with brooding silence and skulking shadows.

With a cold shiver of apprehension Tex lurched past Cæsar's Bar and Paul's. She felt as if eyes watched from yawning black doorways, darkened windows—eyes that were hostile, suspicious, sinister.

She hugged her beaded bag under her left arm, her right hand clasped over it, and felt the reassuring hardness of the small, snub-nosed pistol, with its Maxim silencer, as it snuggled securely within the torn lining.

She turned into the dimly lighted entrance of the San Francisco Cantina and stumbled up the cheaply carpeted stairs to her room. She closed the door with a bang and hiccoughed as she switched on the light. From under lowered lids she made a hasty survey of the small, bare room, then flung herself full-length on the bed, her purse held tightly across her breast.

ONE HOUR CRAWLED by on furtive, dragging feet. Two. And still Tex lay on her springless wooden bed, feigning drunken slumber.

A slight breeze riffled in through the window stirring the sagging lace curtain to shake some of its dust in Tex's nose. She suppressed a sneeze and turned it into a snore with a choked sort of snort on the end of it.

A little longer she listened to the swishing of the curtain as it flapped wearily in and out of the window. Then she thought she heard another sound. A shuffling sound, soft, guarded, muffled.

Slowly she sat up, swinging her feet quietly over the edge of the bed and eased them to the carpetless floor. Silently she crept across the room to the door and paused, tensing, listening, her bead bag clutched in her right hand.

At first there was nothing—just silence—then a faint hissing sound. Tex leaned nearer to the crack and a few whispered words drifted in to her.

"But, Señor Jefe, she ees wan of my percentage girls. Mucho good wan, too. You make wan beeg mistake. She ees not what you t'ink." The voice was Pancho's—Pancho of the *Blue Fox*.

"Well, I ain't takin' no chances. She talks like that Texan female dick.... Anyway—we'll leave him for her."

In her startled surprise Tex lost the rest of the sentence. She gripped the bead bag more tightly. Damn that Texas drawl of hers! For a second she wished she had heeded her chief's warning and brought Bobbie with her. Then she laughed softly, a shaky little laugh. She'd been in tight corners before since she'd entered the secret service four years ago, and through her quick wit and clear reasoning she had always managed to extricate herself—with honors—and part of the trapped underworld. That was why the chief had chosen her to unravel the skein of mystery that tangled around the strange death of Melville Hewett, a wealthy San Francisco merchant, and the disappearance of his son, Arthur. The Eel had been seen coming out of Hewett's home the night before the murder.

Tex was suddenly aware of a curious absence of sound. She waited a moment, holding her breath, her left hand on the door-knob. Then with a swift, cat-like movement, she pulled the door toward her. It opened abruptly, as if someone were pushing against it. She flashed her hand inside her bag, her fingers closing around the pistol, but suddenly recoiled with a stifled cry as a man's body plunged inward and fell forward on his face.

There was something peculiar about his swollen, twisted limbs. Something that vaguely reminded Tex of another man. Who was it? Then in a flash she knew. Melville Hewett had looked that same way.

With a revulsion of feeling toward touching anything lifeless, that she had never been able to overcome, she turned the man on his back.

Staring up at her with glassy eyes, with the contorted features of one who has died in agony, was Bobbie; Bobbie, who was the youngest member of the department and whom the chief had evidently sent to protect her.

Tex straightened, her eyes clouded with unexpected tears, and her heart felt sick. Bobbie was such a youngster. So straight and clean. Damn them! Her hot Texan blood began to boil. She'd get them for this!

She leaned over him again, examining him more closely, pondering. There were no marks of violence. No blood. Then the glint of a green circlet on his left wrist caught her eye. The bracelet was of jade, carved, Chinese. Attached to it by a slender gold chain was a small folded paper. Tex stiffened, for instinctively she knew it was a message for her. She spread the paper out and read the illiterate, scribbled words—*"Ull git yuse next if u dont lay off."* At the end, instead of the signature, was a green seal. Tex scrutinized it intently, her eyes narrowing as she turned the paper around. The seal evolved into a bracelet as she examined it. A bracelet with the head of a snake and the tail of a fish. She smiled, a grim twisting of her painted lips. The Eel was an egomaniac. He couldn't resist the temptation of becoming his own press agent.

A low, husky sound issued from the slim, round throat of Tex; a cry of comprehension, relentless rage, warning.

THROUGH THE CROOKED back streets of Old Town, Tex slid cautiously, like some stalking shadow, through streets that seemed to be winding, dirt-smeared menaces leading into oblivion.

She was following her hunch. A hunch that beckoned her to Pancho's crumbling adobe that crouched, like some hunted animal in the treacherous sands of the desert, one mile south of Tia Juana.

From time to time she glanced nervously over her shoulder. Silence trailed back of her—heavy, oppressive. And before her? Nameless peril. A little demon of fear clutched at her heart, squeezing it until she could hardly breathe. A peculiar tingling sensation ran along her arms and twitched the ends of her fingers. She knew the symptoms. She had had the same feeling when she was about to take off for the five-foot hurdles back in Texas. A breathless sort of feeling. A feeling that a hunter must have just before the kill.

Pancho's adobe loomed unexpectedly before her, a darker shadow in the surrounding gloom. It was long, low and narrow. A wide chimney of rotting stones in the back; two thick, weather-scarred doors of solid wood in front; a narrow, deep-set window near the slanting mud roof at either end. No sound came from the adobe and no light penetrated the thick wooden openings.

Tex crept up to the door nearer her and gently pushed against it. It gave silently under her weight. Quickly, quietly she stepped into the long, low-ceilinged room into which it directly opened, her bead bag hugged under her left arm. She blinked at the sudden light although it was only a feeble flicker from three tallow candles that hung in a rusty iron chandelier suspended from a single wooden beam that ran the length of the room.

Swiftly she took in her surroundings. In a shrouded corner was a cot with something moaning under a pair of soiled blankets. Near it drooped the girl with the bracelets, sobbing softly in a suppressed sort of hopelessness.

Tex closed the door quietly and advanced toward the cot.

At the slight sound of her steps the girl looked up, her eyes widening in terror, her narrow white hands flying to her mouth to stifle the cry that sprang to her lips, the bracelets crowding together, clicking, clanking. Then the fear slowly faded from the girl's face. "Oh, it's—you," she said dully.

Tex nodded and grinned. "Sure." She slid a little nearer and stared down at the white face on the pillow. "Arthur Hewett," she whispered. "Doped and kept doped for days," she added to herself.

At that the girl seemed to waken as from heavy stupor. "How did you know? Who are you?" She sprang up facing Tex.

Tex thought rapidly. She must move cautiously—and—quickly. The girl was suspicious, yet Tex felt that through her she would gain the key to the mystery.

"He looks like his pitcher, don't he?" Tex answered the first question, ignoring the second. She lolled against the burnt brick wall, swinging her bag back and forth, searching furtively the other three corners of the room. "Gotter swig er hooch round this heah dump?" she finally asked, turning back to the girl.

The girl shook her head, slumping back into the chair, her long fingers playing nervously with her bracelets.

"Now, ain't that too bad?" murmured Tex, watching her from under lowered lids. "My, ain't them bracelets pretty?" She stretched an experimental hand toward the girl's left wrist.

The girl drew back sharply, alarm in her shadowed eyes, her fingers curling protectively around the eight circlets.

Tex assumed a sullen tone. "Ah—what'd'yuh take me fur? A cheap dip?" She glanced toward the two doors. "Hell! Ah'd give mah best gold inlay fur a shot er hooch."

A pale little smile hovered around the girl's lips. "I'm sorry—but there isn't any here—only—" She chopped her sentence off abruptly with a little gasp of fright.

"Only what?" prodded Tex quietly, successfully cloaking

her eagerness. "If thar's anything that'll take the place—er hooch—hand it ovah, honey, 'cause Ah'm lower than a snake's hips."

"Snakes!" whispered the girl in deadly fear, and Tex leaned toward her suddenly.

"Gawd! Thar ain't no snakes—heah?" Under the pretense of dismay she studied the girl intently. Snakes? The deaths of Hewett and Bobbie strangely resembled the deadly bites of rattlers. The swollen limbs; the discolored flesh; the almost invisible twin red marks on the left wrists. And yet there had been no snakes.

The girl recovered herself and regarded Tex a little doubtfully. "No—no—of course not." She turned to soothe the moaning man with gently caressing hands, the bracelets huddling down toward her slender hand. She turned back to Tex. "How did you know of this place?" she demanded unexpectedly, a sharp note in her usually low tones.

Tex didn't answer at once. Instead she hitched a little nearer to the bed, keeping her back to the wall, facing the two doors. "Listen, honey," she murmured at last, "Ah come heah to help you." A crooning note slid into her throaty voice and she glanced significantly toward the wasted form of Arthur Hewett.

The girl's eyes followed hers and returned, poignant pain suffusing their shadowed depths. She gazed up at Tex, hesitating, seeming to consider.

And Tex waited, outwardly calm, in no hurry. Inwardly at a high-pitched, nervous tension, her ears cocked for any outside disturbance, her eyes darting to the doors, the windows, around the room, back to the girl and the moaning man. If, as she surmised, the girl was weak, guarding some secret, through love—or fear—she would break under Tex's soft persuasion.

"Oh, I'm afraid—afraid." The words were so low Tex had to stoop to catch them.

The girl clasped her hands tightly in her lap and swayed back and forth.

"Afraid of what—of—who?" prompted Tex. Lord, if the girl would only hurry! A cold feeling of playing for time shivered through her. She hugged her bag more closely under her left arm, the fingers of her right hand curling about the broken clasp. Seconds seemed to leap at her—crowding—crowding—

Presently the girl spoke, her words low, halting—as if being dragged through unwilling lips. "Oh, if you could take—Arthur away—away—where it's safe—safe." She stared up at Tex, repeating the last word in a sort of frenzied appeal.

Tex suddenly put out her hand and grasped the girl's left wrist. The bracelets slid away from her fingers, slipping along the girl's arm as if they were something animate—alive.

For an instant the very intensity of her gaze held the girl irresolute, tractable, willing. "Ah'll take Arthur where it's safe—but—first—you must tell me about—these." She gave the girl's arm a little shake before letting go and the bracelets rattled together.

"I—can't. I'm—afraid—" Her voice trailed off into a sobbing whisper.

"For Arthur!" There was a breathless urgency to Tex's guarded tones as her eyes glanced from the doors to the girl and back again.

"For Arthur!" echoed the girl, a curious little trill creeping into her voice. Her teeth bit into her lower lip and her long, thin fingers twined about the bracelets. She looked down at her restless hands while her words jerked out, automatically, as if some irresistible force were driving her. "I came from a little country town—two years ago. I couldn't get work—and—Jefe found me—starving. He planted me in—Melville Hewett's home—as a maid. Then Mr. Hewett made me his ward. I guess he felt sorry for me—and—he was so good to me—I—I—didn't want to go on—but I was afraid—of—Jefe—"

"Go on with what?" interrupted Tex, every faculty strained for the slightest sound of movement from the stillness of the desert. The shadowy room, like herself, seemed to be holding its breath—waiting—waiting—

The girl sent her a lightning glance of doubt, then went on, a new note calming her voice. A note of fatality—resignation. "Go on with the plans to rob Mr. Hewett—then—I—met—Arthur—" She turned her attention to the man on the cot, seeming to forget everything else. "They have kept him under morphine—to try to make him sign—"

"Sign what?" Tex shifted her position a little, her eyes on the doors.

"The paper—that Jefe had drawn up in his own name—"

"Then Arthur inherited his father's fortune?" Tex asked the question out of the side of her mouth. Her vigilance was directed toward an almost inaudible sound just beyond the doors.

"Yes."

"And after he signs they intend to—"

"Yes—yes. Oh, God!" The girl's voice rose to a high key of hysteria.

"Sh—" Tex wheeled on her suddenly, a cautioning finger to

her lips. "Quick! Tell me what you're hiding!" she whispered, her fingers pressing into the girl's arm.

For one pulsating instant the girl hesitated, her eyes as she gazed up at Tex veiled, defiant; then her shadowy lids drooped over them and she slid her bracelets up and down with agitated fingers. "It's—it's—a paper Mr. Hewett made Jefe give him—"

"Where's this paper now?"

"Arthur gave it to me—to hide—"

"Where did you hide it?"

The girl stretched her hands toward Tex in a gesture of desperate entreaty. "Oh, you *will* take Arthur where he'll get well—and be—safe?"

Tex lapsed back into her soft drawl, successfully cloaking her impatience. "Sure, honey, Ah promised, but you didn't tell me where you hid the paper."

"I hid it in—" The girl's eyes widened in terror as they shot past Tex to the doors.

Tex followed her gaze to the door nearest her. Slowly— quietly it was being pushed inward. Tex stiffened impercep- tibly, her bead bag gripped tightly in both hands. Her mouth suddenly went dry and an icy finger seemed to trail along her spine.

Into the dim circle of light slid The Eel, his hands in his pockets, his crafty features set in an oily, unreadable mask.

Pancho followed him, an ugly grin pulling at his thick lips. A sharp-edged stiletto in his hand. "Better keel 'er now, eh, Jefe?" he flung at The Eel in a sort of gloating snarl.

"Naw, not that way, yuh'd get caught bang ter rights an' take a fall to the big house." The Eel stared at Tex, his deep, expres- sionless eyes glittering in the half-light like a snake's.

" 'Lo," ventured Tex, her heart pounding against her side.

Pancho grunted, examining his knife.

The Eel glided toward Tex, a sinister smile stretching his narrow, fish-like mouth. "I got a more artistic way ter bump off them that gets in my way."

Tex's hand slid cautiously into her bag. She could shoot her way out if it was necessary but that would mean defeat. She wanted an explanation of the mystery; a confession if possible. And she felt that The Eel's tremendous ego would be his downfall. He was so cocksure of himself. So confident that he could always squirm from under any police trap set to ensnare him.

Tex forced a laugh through stiff lips. "Say, fellah, who you goin' to bump off—an' if so—why—an'—how?"

The Eel stopped a few feet from her and regarded her with a sly smirk. "Thought yuh'd like a bracelet." He brought his hand out of his pocket, gingerly holding a jade circlet toward her.

A little gasp came from the girl but the two men were too engrossed in watching Tex to heed it.

The Eel came closer, almost touching her arm with the green bangle. She made no move to take it, although an involuntary shudder ran through her body.

"For God's sake, Jefe, don't—don't!" The girl's voice shivered upward into a thin shriek.

He wheeled toward her, a grin that was baleful in its significance twitching his lips. "Aw, don't worry none, sister. I got one fer yuh, too."

The girl shrank further into the shadows, her slim fingers clutching at each other in a frenzy of fear.

Then Tex spoke softly, in a sort of deadly calm, her Texan drawl more noticeable than ever, her greenish gold eyes flashing in the wavering half-light as she held The Eel with her steady stare. "Ah—don't—want—your bracelet. Ah—never—did—like 'em. But—Ah'm kinda curious— What's in 'em?" This last was a random shot but it had the desired effect. She heard the girl's sharp intake of breath; noted the slight movement of startled surprise from Pancho. Her eyes, however, never left The Eel.

No change of expression came over his evil mask of a face. Only a trifle more expansion of his narrow chest. "I don't mind tellin' yuh because yuh ain't goin' ter live long enough ter spill it, see?" He paused dramatically to let this sink in.

Tex merely nodded and presently The Eel went on, wallowing in his own conceit. Tex smiled inwardly.

"*I* invented it, see? The hollow bracelets. First fer smugglin' in dope, then out of my own head popped another idea. Poison, from my friend the rattler. A Chink learned me how ter take it out of the snake." He stopped talking and grinned maliciously, fingering the jade bracelet.

Tex guessed that the "Chink" was himself. She stared at the bracelet, then at him, simulating awe, horror, admiration. "Lordy," she whispered, "It sure takes a heap of *brains* to figure that out!"

He seemed to expand more than ever.

Tex waited, her hand grasping the pistol inside her bag.

The Eel was so absorbed in his own achievement that he didn't notice, and Pancho's mind was diverted, watching The Eel in fascinated horror, his stiletto in his belt.

There was no movement from the girl and Tex wondered what she was doing. She didn't dare look, take her vigilant attention from Jefe. The green bangle made her feel creepy, as if a snake were actually crawling over her body. She moistened her dry lips with the tip of her tongue and forced herself a step nearer The Eel.

Instantly Pancho lunged toward her, his hand flashing to his dagger.

"Aw, lay off, will yuh," Jefe snapped irritably. "Put up yuh jack-knife." He again addressed himself to Tex. "Now I'll show yuh how I put Hewett an' yuh little dick friend out of the way." He turned the bracelet around carefully and pointed to two sharpened gold points on the inside. "Them," he explained, "represents the fangs, an' when pushed onter the arm it releases this little spring, stabbin' the flesh at the same time and the poison pours inter the holes, see?" A maniacal laugh fell from his twisting lips.

Tex shivered.

"An' yuh don't like bracelets?" He turned to the girl with a sinister grin. "But Mame here does. Don't yuh, Mame?"

The girl gave a cry of terror.

Pancho laughed and at a signal from The Eel sprang in front of Tex, grasping the girl around the waist, pinioning her wildly fighting arms to her sides and propelling her toward the advancing Jefe.

"I'll show yuh how it works," bragged The Eel, looking at Tex over his shoulder. "Then yuh'll know in advance just how yuh'll act, see?" He gripped the girl's wrist.

She wriggled and jerked in a panic of fear. "Don't! Don't!" She turned tragic, horror-stricken eyes to Tex. "For God's sake, stop him!"

Tex stood motionless, her heart thumping against her chest, her eyes riveted on the green bracelet.

The Eel paused and thrust his evil face close to the girl's. "Hand over that paper an' I'll let yuh off."

"What paper?" the girl parried faintly.

"Yuh know what paper! The one Hewett took off of me."

The girl hesitated, her apprehensive eyes darting about the room. When at last she spoke it seemed to Tex that the words were meant for her. "The—the—one where you admitted killing Hewett's partner—and threatened to kill Hewett—in the same way—if he refused to give you one hundred thousand dollars? Well—I—I—destroyed it."

"Yuh lyin'! Come clean or—" The Eel held the bracelet close to her face.

A little moan trembled from her lips and she tried to pull away; then suddenly she lifted her head and looked at The Eel squarely with a pathetic show of bravado. "Yes—I have—the—paper—but—I won't give it to you!—I promised—Arthur." The last word was a faint whisper, almost a prayer, and the thought flashed through Tex's seething mind that this girl, weak, misguided, had somehow gained a noble strength through her love for Arthur Hewett.

With his thin lips stretched over his teeth in a half snarl, The Eel sprang at the girl, grasping her wrist while Pancho laughed and held her waist with his great hairy hands.

"Yuh last chance, yuh fool," hissed Jefe. "Hand over that paper!"

The girl seemed to wilt, her head drooping forward as if too heavy to hold erect, although her words rang out clearly in the silently waiting room. "No! You—murderer!"

"Hold her arm out, Pancho," ordered Jefe, and the green bangle touched her slender clenched hand.

"Oh, God! Oh, God!" she murmured hopelessly, despairingly.

Tex eased a little to one side so that Pancho's broad back was between her and the girl.

"She's too good ter live," continued The Eel, and laughed. A sound that reminded Tex of a hyena she had once heard in the zoo—mirthless, blood-chilling.

Then with his laugh another sound mingled—slyly apologetic. A sort of muffled plop.

An expression of wonder spread over Pancho's crafty features as he loosened his hold on Mame and slumped grotesquely to the brick floor.

"What the hell?" muttered The Eel, staring at the inert body of Pancho; then he raised his eyes to a thin stream of smoke that was drifting from the mouth of a small pistol encased in Tex's steady fingers. His gaze traveled on upward until it encountered the unflinching gold-green eyes of Tex.

"Ah'd—rather take you—alive," she murmured with a faint smile.

For a moment he stared at her, expressionless, immovable; then without the slightest warning he sprang straight at her, knocking the pistol to the floor, curling his fingers about her wrist. Holding the jade bracelet lightly, gingerly, between the thumb and fingers of his right hand.

A little quiver of panic shivered through Tex, then her cold, sane reasoning came to her rescue. She held The Eel's eyes with her own while she eased her left hand toward the green menace and with a swift movement of her strong fingers snatched the bracelet from him. He lunged for it. She met the darting hand with a movement as swift as his own. His slender fingers entered the circlet; the needle-like prongs cut and tore. He gave a cry of rage and terror, clawing frantically at the poisonous manacle, but the more he pulled at it the deeper sank the sharp gold points into his punctured flesh.

His writhing agony was horrible to see. It made Tex a little sick. She stooped to recover her pistol and regarded the girl who sagged against the cot and stared at her with a dazed look in her shadowy eyes.

"In which bracelet did you hide the paper?" asked Tex unexpectedly.

The girl fingered the bangles with fluttering fingers. "This one," she answered automatically, caressing a beautifully carved circlet of mellowed ivory. "It's—Arthur's favorite."

Tex caught the girl by her shoulders and gently shook her. "Gather yourself," she admonished, not unkindly, "and go quickly to Tia Juana. Phone to my chief, J.C. Gilbert. Here's his number. Tell him Tex has sent for him. To come to Pancho's at once—and to bring a doctor." She gave the girl a little push toward the door. "Hurry!"

Slowly Mame pulled the heavy door toward her, paused and looked back at Tex with a slight pleading gesture of her slim white hands. "You'll take care of—Arthur?"

Tex nodded, still the girl lingered.

"When he wakes—you'll tell him—that—my—my—love for him—was greater—than—than—my—fear?"

A lump rose in Tex's throat and she had to swallow it before answering. "Ah'll—tell him," she said softly.

Mame left reluctantly, slipping quietly out into the darkness, closing Tex in the shrouded room.

The candles burned low, dripping over the edges of their rusty iron holders.

Tex allowed her eyes to wander around the dimly flickering room, to slide quickly over the lifeless body of Pancho, on to the twisted form of The Eel, that even in death seemed to coil, like a snake. She turned with a lightening spirit to Arthur Hewett. He was breathing evenly, calmly.

She dropped wearily into the chair near the cot and slipped her pistol back into the frayed depths of her bead bag. Her fingers touched the cool hardness of a pair of handcuffs. "Bracelets," she murmured, and a little exultant cry trickled from her throat.

White Talons

Tex follows a hunch.

TEX SLID INTO the vacant chair at the roulette wheel. The Foreign Club was brilliant, whose slightly aloof atmosphere appealed to the mass of unrelated humans who storm the hooch gates of Tia Juana—restless seekers of thrills; fugitives; oily Mexicans—driftage.

Tex allowed her eyes to rove aimlessly around the immense gambling casino, noting, with a little glow of excitement, the crowded bars that flanked the four sides of the room, and the gaming tables—chuck-a-luck; black-jack, roulette.

Her eyes came slowly back to the slant-eyed, flat-nosed Chinaman who sat on her right at the roulette wheel, then shifted to the nervously eager flapper on her left. Tex's first impulse was to speak to the girl, but she checked herself. Some uncanny sixth sense warned her to watch—and wait. She placed a modest coin on the first dozen and turned her attention to the croupier.

He was a man of about forty, tall, gaunt, with an air of mystery in his burning black eyes that intensified the pallor of his long, narrow face. His arms hung loosely from his shoulders, like those of a gorilla. There was something about his appearance that, to Tex, created the impression of a man hiding some deformity. Just what that deformity was Tex didn't know. It was something elusive, haunting—sinister.

She watched his hands as they spun the wheel, cognizant of the flexible fingers that were slim, tapering, white.

Her eyes dropped to her own hands as they rested lightly

in her lap beneath the table. And a gratified gleam flashed momentarily in the green-gold of her eyes. They were small, well-kept hands, burned a rich tan from the sun. The fingers that were vital and slightly spatulate. Strong, capable hands they were. She eased one now into the inside pocket of her plaid sport coat and felt the security of her blunt-nosed pistol with its Maxim silencer. But she hoped she wouldn't have to use it.

There was a slight, almost imperceptible movement beside her and instinctively she knew that the Chinese was regarding her out of obscurely suspicious eyes.

Her glance shifted slowly upward as far as the green felt of the table-top and there rested for a moment on those strange white hands of the croupier—hands that seemed to hover—to haunt, filling her with a vague sense of foreboding—and of some faint memory.

With an unhurried gesture of unconcern that she was far from feeling, Tex drew a small gold compact from her pocket. She snapped it open, removed the miniature puff and carelessly powdered her short, straight nose. She tilted the tiny mirror and cocked her head, not looking at her own reflection but at that of the feverish-eyed girl who sat on her left.

A 1928 flapper of the latest, most daring model—thick blonde hair cut shoulder length; ridiculously tight two-piece sport frock with the skirt a little above the knees; straight bare legs with wool socks wrinkled artistically over the ankles. She was painted like a Border percentage girl. Flapper to the last mascaraed eyelash, thought Tex—yet there was a difference—she didn't smoke.

The little gold compact was replaced in its obscure hiding

place beside the pistol as Tex rose with a slight stir of excitement and leaned toward the roulette wheel. "Come on—you—red," she gurgled in her throaty Texan drawl and placed a five-dollar bill on 25.

The wheel spun around with its peculiar whirring sound, reminding Tex of a person breathing rapidly. The little white ball danced madly within its confined circle, clicking, clacking until it gradually lost momentum and with a final satisfied plop settled itself into the groove between 2 and 17.

Tex reached for her winnings and her fingers encountered those of the croupier. The contact sent a chill of apprehension through her and she felt suddenly that this man's hidden deformity was not of the body but of the mind. There was something eerie, death-like in the feel of his clammy flesh.

She moistened her lips and forced herself to laugh. A sound that was more like a crow than a laugh.

"Señorita ees lucky, *esta noche, si?*" The croupier's voice was a soft purr.

"Squeeze out your tears, Spanish, Ah know mah onions," grinned Tex. Her glance slid quickly from the man's inscrutable face to the girl's, surprising a sudden gleam of defiance—or was it jealousy?—in her bold blue eyes. Tex wondered. She wouldn't be so easy to handle, decided Tex, after a hasty, though thorough, inspection of this opinionated flapper.

Tex glanced at her wrist-watch. It was nearly closing time. A frenzied last whir of the wheel. Cashing of final bets. Scraping of chairs. Voices. High-pitched. Deep. Garbled with too much Border hooch. Noise, confusion—then—silence.

Tex sauntered to the door and looked out into the dimly lighted main street; a street that crouched like some skulking

alley cat when the long gray shadows presaged the coming of night. An icy finger seemed to trail along her spine before she turned and regarded the flapper with assumed surprise. "Say, honey, the Border is closing right soon."

The girl stared back at her with hostile eyes. "Well, what of it?" she answered.

"Nothin', honey—only—it's kinder dangerous to hang round Tia Juana—after—dark." Tex smiled lazily at the girl, albeit she felt the eyes of the croupier observing her with distrust and a veiled sort of cunning.

The girl twitched her narrow shoulders. "It might be a good idea to mind your own business," she retorted.

Tex shrugged and turned back to the door. Outwardly calm, indifferent. Inwardly, her clever brain was working rapidly— planning. This wise-eyed flapper was Margaret Gaylor, sixteen-year-old daughter of Paul Gaylor, well-known capitalist of Los Angeles. A week ago she had been reported missing and the chief had put Tex on the case. And Tex, following one of her common-sense hunches, had trailed her to Tia Juana.

"Better step on the gas, sister, or you'll miss the last choo-choo for San Diego." Margaret Gaylor was saying, and she laughed, a shrill, go-to-hell laugh.

Then a soft, purring voice slid into her brittle tones. "Señorita ees staying with *mia madre*—" The Spaniard paused, spreading out his white hands in a gesture, eloquent—suggestive.

"Is zat so? Now, ain't that just—swell? Well, s'long." Tex turned again to the door, undecided, wary.

Her car was the last to nose its way over the Border. It was a car whose nondescript black body cleverly camouflaged its high-powered motor and melted easily into shadows. She speeded up to thirty as she crossed to American soil and kept her foot on the throttle until she had covered a mile of highway. Gradually she slowed, idling along at ten—five—listening, but nothing followed her save silence—profound, disturbing.

She turned the car off the road, shifted into neutral and slid to a noiseless stop. For some time she sat quietly, leaning on the steering wheel, waiting—pondering. She had found Margaret Gaylor and the girl had plainly shown that she had left home of her own free will. Resented anyone interfering. It would be easy for Tex to report to her chief in San Francisco. Notify Paul Gaylor and let him go after his own daughter. Yet Tex hesitated. Some invisible wire was pulling her back. Intuition urged her to return. Was the girl in danger? The vision of two long white hands rose before her eyes. She had seen those white hands before. Where? Something tugged at the warm, dauntless heart of Tex. She waited—waited—until dark night came with its stealthy tread.

Cautiously she stepped to the ground. Slipping along through the shadows, she edged around dust-smeared cacti, murky sagebrush until at last she reached the sordid rear entrance of Tia Juana. She hurried along the narrow back roads—roads that reminded Tex of menacing shrouds—and turned into a short alley that ended abruptly in the looming shadow of the croupier's adobe.

Nervously she looked around. Fear perched on her shoulder. Something was creeping silently behind her. She turned and waited, her fingers curling around the butt of her gun, her heart pounding in her throat.

The thing crept nearer—nearer—and still Tex waited. It straightened suddenly, evolving into the slant-eyed, flat-nosed Chinese. He held something in his hand—something long and thin and curved, that glinted like a narrow thread of light in the surrounding gloom.

Tex spoke then, huskily—a little unsteadily. "Stop! Or—Ah'll—shoot the works!"

The man paused. "You no shoot. Too muchie noise. Bling boss," he said and lunged at her.

Tex heard the faint swish of a knife as it flashed upward past her cheek. She sprang backward. There was a slight apologetic cough and the Chinese pitched forward—heavily—silently.

Tex held her breath, listening, peering around in the darkness, but there was nothing—no one. She slid the pistol back in her coat pocket and smiled grimly. Then the croupier *had* feared her—expected her— And the thought came to her more forcibly than ever that Margaret Gaylor, through her worldly ignorance, her love of adventure, had deliberately walked into danger, had fallen into a trap that had been cunningly laid for her arrogant, thrill-hunting feet. Undoubtedly she had been fascinated by the man with the strange, hypnotic eyes and slender white hands, and had followed those slyly evil, beckoning fingers. Where had Tex seen those white talons before? She cudgeled her brain but the answer to the riddle persistently eluded her.

She knew the crumblingly artistic adobe the croupier lived in as she knew every other moldy dump in the wicked little Mexican town. She also knew that the croupier lived alone with his slant-eyed, flat-nosed Chinese servant. But here her information ran into a blank wall. He had come to Tia Juana a year ago—from where no one seemed to know, nor care. Neither did she—until now.

At the door of the adobe Tex hesitated. Her mouth went dry and she had difficulty in swallowing. She kept her right hand tucked in the inside pocket of her coat and lifted the rusty iron knocker with her left. Up and down she jerked it, listening to its deadened rap as it echoed hollowly through the gloomy interior. Stillness followed. Stillness that seemed to pound on her eardrums.

Cautiously she tried the heavy latch and pushed against the door. It opened easily. Almost too easily, thought Tex.

Her keen eyes endeavored to pierce the gray dimness of the room she entered, for she felt instinctively that this abode of the mysterious croupier would be more difficult to leave than it had been to enter.

She slid noiselessly over the stone floor to a low doorway at the farther end of the room—and—paused, her left hand on the knob. A moment longer she hesitated. Then she pulled the massive door toward her.

There was a furtive, unexpected movement behind her. A maniacal chuckle and she was propelled with stunning force into the shrouded void before her.

A slight click sounded. Tex swung around. The thick door had closed. In the sudden, rather terrifying darkness, Tex fumbled for the knob, but she knew before she tried it that the door was locked from the outside.

The air was dank and smelt of dead things.

"Damn!" swore Tex. She had left her flashlight in the car.

"Oh! Thank God!" The voice floated through the gloom in a sort of muffled gasp.

"Thank *me*—you mean—you damn—little—idiot!" retorted Tex irritably, trying to pierce the enveloping darkness. "Where in hell—*are* you?"

"Here," came faintly from one corner.

"Ah cain't see you—so you better come to me, your eyes bein' more used to the dark."

There was a moment's silence, then, "I—I—can't—"

"Cain't? What's the matter? Are you tied?"

"N-no—but—but—I'm—afraid—"

"Escared? Of what?" Tex stared around her nervously, clutching her gun.

"Of—of—crawling things—I think—I think—they're—rats!" Margaret's voice ended in a little shriek.

Tex felt her hair bristle on her head like a frightened cat's tail. And her eyes, becoming more accustomed to the unlighted room, made out two tiny torches that glittered in the blackness. Something scuttled over her feet. She glanced around her. In every direction she looked there were eyes. Eyes that seemed to watch—to wait—expectantly.

"Gawd! How many are—theah?"

Margaret's voice came to her thinly—unevenly—as if she had been crying. "I think there—m-must be a m-million.

Oh—I'm so fr-frightened!"

Unconsciously Tex slid her feet along the dirt floor toward the girl. Her toes curling spasmodically at each step. She had a horror of treading on any of those squirming, worm-like tails.

Margaret clutched her arm when at last she reached her. "You'll—you'll—get me out of this—won't you?" Her tone was pleading, helpless. Gone was her worldly swagger, her insolent assurance. She was like a terrified child, whimpering for protection. Tex could hear the little nervous click of her teeth as she snapped them together.

Tex didn't answer at once. Her mind was reaching for a half-formulated plan. "How long you been heah?" she finally asked.

"I—don't—know. It seems ages." She paused and Tex could feel her shivering body as she leaned against her. Tex waited.

Presently the girl went on. "He brought me here tonight. Said he wanted to show me—some—some—old Spanish heirlooms." She caught her breath on a half sob. "Of course—of course—I came."

"M'm," grunted Tex. Silence followed, then. "Did you notice any other entrance to this heah dump?"

"There isn't any. Just the door—we came through. He told me—" Margaret's voice trailed off into a stifled wail.

"Now, ain't that just—swell." Tex's tone was sober. She felt sober. She didn't relish the thought of dying by inches of starvation—or—thirst—or both. Her characteristic shrug slid into a shiver. "Spill everything, kid," she said. Perhaps while the girl was talking she could figure out some plan, some means of escape.

The girl was silent so long that Tex grew impatient "Make it snappy! Ah ain't so wild 'bout this heah rat-hole." She spoke gruffly, her mind alert, her ears cocked for the least variation in the sound of the rodents—scuttling, gnawing, waiting. Her eyes darted around the four corners of the room, trying to see more than thick shadows and gleaming eyes. "Step on it kid."

"I—I—don't know where to begin."

"You might try startin' at the beginnin' fur a change," suggested Tex.

"I really don't see that your silly questions will help me to get out of here—"

"Us," corrected Tex with a grim twisting of her lips. Then she grasped the girl's arm and shook her. "Listen, sister, this ain't the place to high-hat me. Spit it out—an' spit it out pronto." She shook her again. "Why did you run away from home?"

At that the girl seemed to wilt. "Oh, I—I—" she began and halted.

Tex shifted nervously from one foot to the other. Her brain was circling madly. God! What was the matter with her? Why couldn't she think? The air seemed to choke—to depress her. The stench of rotting dead things seemed to be getting worse. It nauseated her. To be caught like a rat in a trap. A rat in a trap! She had faced death many times since she'd entered the secret service—but—God! she'd always had a fighting chance!

Margaret's voice droned wearily on, finally penetrating Tex's seething thoughts, clearing them again—bringing back her sane reasoning, her dogged determination to outwit fate—or the devil behind this particular one.

"I—I—was bored to tears with the pocket-flask sheiks," the girl was saying, "and longed for a new thrill—"

"Yeah, all flappers long fur new thrills—"

"And—and—then I came to Tia Juana with some friends and saw—Tony—"

"Tony?"

"Yes, Tony, the croupier. At first I only noticed his hands. They fascinated me. They were so white—and—slim— What was that?" Margaret stopped with a little gasp.

Tex peered through the gloom. "Nothin' but another one of those damn rats. They're hungry, poor things—an' waitin' fur us to croak." This attempt at humor had a peculiar effect on Margaret.

"My God! That's what *he* said!" Her voice rose to a high pitch of hysteria.

Tex dug her strong fingers into the girl's arm. "Sh—" she cautioned.

They listened a moment, scarcely breathing, tense—apprehensive. Then Tex went on rapidly in a whisper. "Then Tony made love to you an' urged you to come heah with his mah to chaperon—"

"How did you know?" asked Margaret wonderingly.

Tex smiled in the darkness. "Ah get paid fur knowin'—things," she answered noncommittally. "But that's all Ah do know. Go on from theah."

"Until tonight he was wonderful—then he told me— Oh, it's too horrible—" Margaret began to sob softly, hopelessly.

"Go on," snapped Tex impatiently.

The next words came out brokenly, in a jerky sort of whisper. "He—he—told me—that my father had sent the ransom money as he had directed—but—but—he wasn't going to send me back—until—after—after—I—was—dead—and—and—the rats had—had—eaten—my pretty—face—" She ended with a muffled groan, slumping forward, her head in her arms.

Tex shook her. "Did he say anything else?"

"N-no—yes—no. I don't—know."

Tex gripped her by the arm and yanked her to her feet. "Think!" she commanded. "Think—fast!"

"Yes—yes—he said something—about—always hugging his—sweeties—to death—"

Hugging his sweeties to death! Tex stiffened. It came to her in a flash. Just where she'd seen those flexible white hands. The long pale hands of the Strangler! Wanted in a dozen States for as many murders—always girls! Young, pretty girls. The Strangler whom no one had ever seen—except those poor dead creatures; who had cleverly erased every possible clue. But Tex had a remarkable memory for details. She had seen those hands before—choking a cat. She shuddered now as the picture of the animal's agonizing struggles rose before her. The man wore a wide-brimmed hat and as he was stooping over, his face was hidden. She had called out to him, remonstrating. He had ducked and vanished. But the memory of those cruel white fingers had never left her.

A shiver of misgiving seized her. God! She wasn't dealing with a criminal alone, but a madman as well! She gripped her pistol a little more tightly and grasped Margaret's hand. "C'm on," she commanded under her breath.

Margaret clung to her, whispering, "What are you going to do?"

"Your friend Tony's comin' back heah, ain't he?" Tex spoke guardedly as they shuffled their feet through the scattering rodents, toward the door.

"I—I—think—so." The girl's voice was quivering—uncertain.

"Well, Ah *know* so. He cain't choke anybody by absent treatment, can he?"

"N-n-n-no." Margaret's teeth were chattering, and out of the corners of her eyes Tex saw the girl's hands fly to her throat as if the fingers of the Strangler were already squeezing it. Her own throat felt rather tight.

At the door Tex fumbled cautiously for the knob and measured off a space to the left and right of the door. She motioned for Margaret to stand on one side while she herself backed against the wall on the other.

"Now listen, kid," was her whispered instruction, "when the boy friend romps in, all set fur the swell death scene—you beat it—savvy?"

Margaret didn't answer. Tex could hear her stifled sobs, and she spoke again, harshly, impatiently. "Did you hear me?"

"Ye-yes," came faintly, "bub-but—what are you—going—to do?"

"Ah'll just naturally make mah way out," answered Tex and there was a little excited gurgle in her whisper.

"Oh, God! Why did I ever run away? Oh, God!" moaned Margaret.

Tex shifted her feet nervously. She thought she heard something moving on the other side of the door. "Say, will you shut up an' snap out of it! An' when this door opens—duck!"

"I—I—can't. I'm—afraid—" The girl's voice trailed off into silence.

Tex swore under her breath. God! If the little idiot pulled a fade-out now! "Say, do you know what—g-u-t-s—spells?" she gritted.

The girl stirred slightly and Tex imagined that she had lifted her head, straightened her shoulders.

"Of—course—I do." A small semblance of the old arrogance crept back into the girl's low tone.

Tex smiled in the darkness. "Well, have you got any?" she inquired disagreeably.

There was a slight pause, then, "Certainly, I've got—guts."

"You gotter show me," muttered Tex.

Margaret's voice grew stronger, louder—"Oh, I will. I will! I'll do anything you say. I'll—"

"Sh—" cautioned Tex.

She felt, rather than heard, a faint scraping and suddenly the restless rats became quiet—motionless, their beady little eyes fixed. They seemed to sense, as she had, some hidden danger. She listened—waiting. Every faculty strained.

Abruptly the darkness was stabbed with a thin rapier of light that gradually widened as the door crept open like some stealthy ghost. Then the light became blurred by a shadow. The shadow of the Strangler.

Tex heard Margaret's sharp intake of breath, as if she had shut off her involuntary cry with her hand. Tex's eyes slid swiftly down the man's dangling arm and in horrified fascination she watched those long, narrow fingers as they curled and uncurled in his palms, reminding her of the huge feelers of an octopus. Fear caught at her heart. There was something so savagely fatal about the thin pointed tips.

She gave herself a little mental shake and a soft, husky laugh gurgled up through her slim, round throat.

At the unexpected sound the croupier wheeled in her direction. Blinking in the half-light, trying to focus his evil black eyes: "You t'ink you fool me," he said, and there was a gloating sneer in his slurring tones. "You change the face—maybe—but eet not so easy to change the voice."

Tex made no verbal answer to this, but wordlessly she was damning that unmistakable Texas dialect of hers. It had betrayed her before in its subtle personality.

The croupier was speaking again. "You have a pretty throat, too. I like—preety—throats—" The last word was drawn out like the spit of a cat.

Tex kept her back to the wall, edging imperceptibly toward Tony and the open door. "Make a break fur it," she called out suddenly.

The Strangler stiffened and for a moment his hands ceased their spasmodic workings. He stared at Tex—undecided, suspicious. His thick lips stretched back from his teeth in a half snarl.

Margaret sprang for the door, pausing to call over her shoulder. "But you—"

"Beat it!" answered Tex from the side of her mouth. Her eyes on the Strangler, unwavering, deadly calm, her strong fingers gripped about the butt of her pistol.

Still Margaret stood hesitant.

"I can't leave you," she said stubbornly.

Then like writhing serpents the Strangler's hands reached out quickly, his fingers coiling around the girl's throat.

She gave a terrified, gasping cry and clawed frantically, impotently, at those squeezing talons.

Tex leveled but didn't dare press the trigger. The Strangler was swift as a panther—warily cunning.

Tex crept nearer, a dawning horror darkening her eyes. A queer sinking sensation in the pit of her stomach. The girl was no longer struggling. Her arms dangled limply. Her knees sagged.

And just above her lolling blonde head, the face of the croupier leered, his ghastly white features contorted—smeared with blood where the girl had dug her frenzied nails.

Tex raised her gun a little. Her hand shook. She gritted her teeth. *She must aim straight.* If she wavered a fraction of an inch? God! Her hand steadied. There was a sudden hoarse pop; a faint odor of burnt gunpowder.

The Strangler's long claws relaxed—let go, and Margaret slumped out of his grasp, her limp body sliding away, against Tex's feet while Tony spun around like his roulette wheel, jerked to one side and pitched forward. His arms spread out in a final gesture of destruction.

Tex leaned over the inert form of the girl, her heart plunging down to zero. Was it too late? Was she done for? She was so horribly silent. Her face was purple. Her eyes bulged. Tex dragged her into the lighted room beyond. She set her up and shook her back and forth. "Gawd, kid, you cain't pull a flop on me now!" There was a strange new note, that sounded like a sob, in her voice. She held Margaret in her arms and stared at her until the very intensity of her gaze seemed to penetrate the wall of blackness in the girl's mind.

"Guts," murmured Margaret through discolored swollen lips.

Tex helped Margaret to her feet, backed up and kicked the door shut, smiling grimly when she heard the fatal click of the latch as it shot into place, stilling forever the white hands of the Strangler.

THROUGH THE SULLENLY dark night Tex and Margaret stumbled, groping—breathless.

Every now and then they glanced nervously over their shoulders. Blackness stretched back of them like a pointing finger, ominous—silent. Before them, over tangled masses of sagebrush and alkaline-spattered cacti, beckoned a thin ribbon of safety—the Border highway.

And waiting within the white circle of light, thrown from the headlights of a powerful gray car, stood the chief.

"You found the missing heiress, I see," he said and his voice was deep.

"An' that ain't all—Ah found," answered Tex enigmatically, slouching over to where her nondescript car was parked. She put her foot on the starter, shifted into gear and slid on to the highway. "Ah'll beat you back to headquarters," she called, and laughed.

The Canine Tooth

Tex, of the Service, plays a hunch

TEX ELBOWED HER way through the milling, eagerly jostling crowd to the edge of the park, on the outskirts of Tia Juana, where the dog races are held—where the long, lean greyhounds bound from spring traps to rush headlong after an electrically propelled rabbit that they never catch.

A shadow darkened the greenish gold of Tex's eyes as she watched the muzzled dogs being led past the judge's stand, by jockeys in flamboyant silks. And Tex's wide humorous mouth twisted into a little grimace of pain. The dogs were so frantically expectant, so thin, so—hungry. She knew the cruel significance of those secure muzzles. If one should fall the others would forget the rabbit and tear the unfortunate weakling to shreds. Not unlike the trampling, surging mass of humans surrounding her, she thought, with an amused inward smile.

Tex forced her eyes to wander unhurriedly over the heterogeneous multitude and shift back again to rest with assumed indifference on the jockeys and their dogs. And presently there came before her view a youth whose narrow face was the color of the putty-hued greyhound he was handling. His startlingly handsome dark eyes were set a bit too close to his sharp, thin nose. His thick lips were sullen, greedy, sneering.

Tex guessed that this must be the Whippet, so called because of his resemblance to the dogs he owned and raced. He was a sly, rapid-fire little moll buzzer who sheiked the sight-gazing, hooch-inspired females of Tia Juana. He had done a three-year jolt at the Big House for a stick-up in Los Angeles, then

drifted down to the Border to take up an honest profession. Going straight, was the report from headquarters. Looking at him, Tex doubted it.

The mechanical rabbit flashed once around the track, under the hungry noses of the dogs, slyly urging them to follow its false trail. The dogs strained at their leashes, snarling. Starving, plunging, frenzied animals racing after a phantom meal for the pleasure of Border thrill-hunters, alcohol maddened humanity. It made Tex a little sick.

The crowd pressed in behind her, politely fighting for first place, noisy, determined. She felt a sudden, stealthy hand snatch at her tan sport bag. Her fingers tightened over its handle and her eyes slid downward. She saw a hand that was pale olive and broad with stubby fingers tipped by brilliant orange nails. Then it darted away.

Her glance shot up a trifle and to the side, until unexpectedly it encountered the insolent black orbs of Cornita, the Mexican dancing girl who entertained at Paul's in Old Town. Old Town is a small Border settlement of ill-repute, just across the bridge from Tia Juana, that spanned a dry, shallow river-bed.

Tex laughed as she regarded the girl. " 'Lo, Cornie, Ah thought somebody was tryin' to snitch mah bag." She watched the Mexican closely, endeavoring to read the painted mask of her face. She was wondering if the girl suspected that she carried her deadly .22 with its Maxim silencer in her innocent-looking sport purse.

Cornita lifted one contemptuous shoulder and her vividly carmined lips pulled back over sharp discolored teeth in an odd sort of smile that somehow reminded Tex of a snarling dog.

"You tink ever-ree wan in the whole of Mexico steal. Bah! You peeg of a Gringo!" She spat at Tex's feet.

Tex's smile became a trifle set. But she had learned through the hard school of the Secret Service to control her fiery Texan temper. The game was to remain cool while the suspects became hopelessly entangled in their own seething emotions. She looked steadily at Cornita, realizing with a slight inward twinge of dismay that it would be difficult to allay the girl's native mistrust.

"You like Tia Juana?" The question came unexpectedly from Cornita. It was a simple enough question and yet Tex got the impression that there was some hidden motive behind the words. She had come to the dog races yesterday for the first time and had sought the acquaintance of the Mexican dancer. The reason was still rather vague in her own mind, but she was following the dictates of one of her common-sense hunches. In some intangible way the Whippet interested her and Cornita was reputed to be the Whippet's Moll.

"Sure. Ah'm loco about this heah dump." Tex turned back to the race track. Her eyes followed the streaking flashes of gray and tan dog flesh, but her clever mind was on the entertainer at her side.

Her glance trailed slowly back to Cornita, and surprised a peculiar veiled expression in the deep, unsafe pools of her eyes. It gave Tex a creepy feeling. She gripped her bag a little tighter.

"Did you bet on the races?" she asked.

Cornita smiled, an odd, virulent smile. "*Si.* I al-ways bet."

"Who do you think owns the fastest hounds?" Tex's drawl gave the impression of casual interest.

The girl's glance pried, questioned, weighed before she answered. "Señor the Whee-peet. Heeze dogs are mucho queek."

"Yeah. Ah noticed that. They seem to be the skinniest." Tex laughed a little, trying to keep the hurt indignation out of her voice. "Not that theah's a helluva lot of difference. They all look—starved."

There was that same cruel twist to the Mexican's painted lips. "*Si. Si.* The less they eat, the more they run." She laughed then. A strident, savage sound that filled Tex with an incipient dread.

Cornita was edging away from her. "*Adios, señorita.* I go back now to Paul's, to dance for the damn' Gringos." She spat and was suddenly sucked into the human vortex.

Tex lost all interest in the dog race although she lingered until the last of the blatant, queerly assorted mob stampeded from the park, and then trailed them unhurriedly to the open-faced cantinas in Old Town. To one not knowing her she appeared to be seeking, rather unconcernedly, the sensory pleasures of the Border. Her leisurely manner camouflaged her keen mind that was groping to place vagrant thoughts in their proper sequence. She was endeavoring to complete an unfinished theory, a shadowy, intangible picture that teased her sane reasoning.

In some unexplained way Tex felt that there was something more than coincidence, underlying the two attacks by a mad dog that yesterday morning had terrorized the citizens of San Diego. The victims were women with modest fortunes, who had been attacked an hour apart and left with horribly gaping throats.

The frantic cry of, "mad dog," echoed and re-echoed through the panic-stricken streets, calling forth the police, urging them on a blind search for the frothing animal that always vanished before it was seen. It left only one tangible clue—tooth-marks. Tex had carefully studied those incisions and with her unusual sense of detail, had noted the peculiarity of the bites. The incisions were deep, pointed, even, with one exception. The mark from what possibly was the left incisor was not so deep. It was jagged as if the tooth had been broken off.

This, with a man's thick, gray leather glove, which Tex had found in the last sufferer's lonely bungalow on the edge of San Diego, near the Border, she had shown to her chief. He had looked rather grave but had only laughed when she had asked permission to follow a hunch.

"My dear Tex, you are going off on a wild goose chase," he had said, to which she had promptly answered, "Nope. Ah'm rompin' off on a wild dog chase." And she had grinned at him, her gamin-like grin, and with his reluctant consent had started on her cloudy trail.

Her slightly baffled thoughts snapped suddenly back to present surroundings. Her eyes focused on the slim, straight shoulders of the Whippet. He slithered, almost imperceptibly, into the blatantly, obvious doorway of Paul's. Tex eased silently in behind him, following him to a small table at the rear of the café. There Cornita was sitting, resting after her exotic, flaming dance and sipping her *tequila*. Eagerly waiting.

Tex was cognizant of the fire in her deep black eyes as they watched the coming of the Whippet. Then they smoldered with undisguised hate when they darted over the Whippet's shoulder and caught Tex's friendly gaze.

The Whippet stopped abruptly and wheeled on Tex. His expression was lowering, malignant.

Tex grinned. "'Lo," she greeted amiably, sliding uninvited into the vacant chair beside Cornita.

The Mexican dancer smiled at her—the smile that Tex was beginning to hate.

The Whippet said nothing and slumped into the seat opposite. His hands were hidden beneath the table.

"The drinks are on me, fellers. Name your poison," gurgled Tex with a cheerfulness she was far from feeling. Her own capable hands were busy with the purse she held firmly in her lap.

The Whippet scowled, "What's the big idea?" he sneered.

"Idea, feller? I won a healthy pile of iron men, bettin' on your skinny-legged coyotes." She leaned over and patted Cornita's bare, olive-tinted arm. "Now, ain't that just—the swellest idea, Cornie?"

Tex pulled out a roll of greenbacks and the man and woman relaxed. Tex smiled inwardly. She motioned to a waiter who was hovering near with an air of expectancy. He took their liquid orders and Tex resumed her friendly chatter.

"Ah'm loco ovah pooches, an' Ah heah you got a nifty bunch."

She was hoping for some change of expression in the Whippet's sullen face. Some signal—some sign of fear, but there was none.

"Yeah," he agreed indifferently and lighted a cigarette.

"Madre d'Dios! They are the fastest in the whole of the country!" vouchsafed Cornita, her black eyes snapping, glittering with a sort of savage excitement.

Tex took a swallow of the potent Mexican drink the waiter had brought her, blinked, gulped and reached for the glass of water. "Maybe some time you'll show 'em to me." The rising inflection made it a question.

"You can see 'em any day at the track," the Whippet answered her, his cigarette dangling precariously from the side of his thick mouth.

"Ah heah you got a breedin' farm. Maybe you'll take me theah—some time?" Her husky drawl held a very mild sort of interest, but she watched him closely. Her heart was thumping with an irregular, excited beat. Did the Whippet start slightly and send a lightning glance toward Cornita—or was Tex's active imagination playing her tricks?

The Whippet chewed nervously on his cigarette. Apparently he was trying to formulate an answer.

Studying him, Tex had a sudden unexplained desire to experiment. The blind trail she had been following seemed to beckon her on. She played with her glass, lifted it to her lips, swallowed and slowly set the glass back on the table. Her motions were deliberate, leisurely, cloaking her restless eagerness. She sighed and her green-gold eyes stared dreamily into space, then wandered back to Cornita—and the Whippet.

"Ah was just wonderin'," murmured Tex, as if the plan had

just come to her, "if—Ah could buy your farm—an' all your pooches—" She left her sentence unfinished—questioning.

The Whippet sat up with a jerk, his cigarette gripped strongly between his teeth.

Tex gazed at him speculatively, her wide mouth set in a friendly grin. From the corner of her eye she saw Cornita lift her left shoulder in her characteristic gesture of contempt, and wondered if the dancer were trying to send the Whippet some sort of signal.

Finally the man laughed. A sound that was half sneer, half anticipation. "Say, you ain't got enough jack to pay for my outfit."

Tex's expression was one of mild disappointment. "Maybe you know of some other guy—that would be willin' to sell me his hounds?"

The Whippet eyed her suspiciously, as if endeavoring to penetrate her game. "I'm the only bird around this place that raises 'em," he stated tersely, slipping his cigarette from one side of his mouth to the other.

"Now—ain't that just—too bad?" Tex paused uncertainly, then leaned across the table. "But if you changed your mind— how much would you take?"

"Twenty-five thousand—cash," snapped the Whippet unexpectedly.

Tex's under-cover smile was grim, tempered with humor. She had a reasonable hunch why the Whippet had added that last word. She pulled her face into a mask of dubious consideration. "Well—that was more than Ah thought of payin'—but—" Her glance slid from one to the other.

The Whippet leered at her.

Cornita smoked in silence, watching him as if waiting for some sign.

Tex eased her hand inside her bag, her strong brown fingers curling around the butt of her .22. If they made any kind of threatening motion, the soft little pop from her pistol would hardly be noticed in the confusion of other noises. She continued in her slow, throaty tones. "Poor old pa left me fifty-thou' an' Ah figgered Ah'd like to invest half of it in somethin'—" Her voice trailed off. Her eyes lowered, although she didn't miss the quick exchange of glances between the Mexican and the Whippet. She rose leisurely and slouched against the table. "If Ah bring the jack tomorrow—will you show me the place?"

The man answered from one side of his mouth, the butt of his cigarette dangling from the other. His handsome dark eyes stared not at her but at the table where her right hand rested. "Meet us here tomorrow—after the races. Bring the cash and we'll take you out to the place."

Tex's glance shifted rapidly to Cornita. The dancer was smiling her evil smile. Tex shivered. A feeling of impending danger gripped her, but she jerked out a cryptic smile of her own that included them both. "Ah'll be heah. S'long." She sauntered toward the doorless entrance and out into the one main street—the street with its surface atmosphere of innocuous carnival and its undercurrent of slinking wolves.

She eased under the steering wheel of her black, inconspicuous car, whose outward appearance belied its swift, powerful motor, and idled slowly past the Customs. Grinning her gamin grin at the hard-boiled American officers on one side—fluttering her expressive eyes at the sheik-like Mexicans on the other.

They inspected her machine, twirled their black mustaches, flourished their six-shooters.

Tex pressed the throttle and shot over the Line, darting like an unsuspected truck horse past the long row of cars and on toward San Diego. Nothing but speed could relieve the excitement that raced like an electric current through her slim, rather boyish young body, and tingled at the ends of her supple brown fingers. Her nostrils distended like a pointer's—on the scent. She wasn't quite sure just what that scent was, but she had all the unmistakable signs of her uncanny sixth sense working frantically around inside of her.

Not until she neared San Diego did she drop back to 40—30—25, curbing her impatience to talk to her chief in San Francisco, although on this particular case of her own choosing he would probably tell her that she was allowing her imagination to run wild.

She gave a nervous little shrug of her shoulders and pulled up in front of a public pay station.

SLOUCHING THROUGH THE cheaply sensational entrance of Paul's the following day, Tex had a little misgiving. Was she following a blind trail after all? Getting herself entangled in something that didn't exist—or that the Secret Service wouldn't be interested in? Jerry Gilbert's voice over the wire had been coolly amused—and just the least bit annoyed. Tex hated to disappoint the chief—and yet some inner voice urged her on. She couldn't turn back now, even if her shadowy deductions led her into embarrassing emptiness.

The stench of sour booze, stale tobacco smoke, perspiring humanity, assailed her nostrils, giving her an odd, sickening sensation in the pit of her stomach.

She paused in the middle of the dance floor and waited for Cornita and the Whippet to reach her.

The dancer stretched her full, carmined lips over her pointed teeth in her menacing smile, her orange-tipped fingers fiddling with an unlighted cigarette. *"Buenas tardes, señorita,"* she greeted pleasantly enough, but Tex read suspicion, hate, in the smoldering black eyes.

" 'Lo," she said to Cornita and turned her attention to the Whippet. He was smiling, and in that smile his thick mouth lost some of its sullenness—its brutal greediness. Then she looked into his eyes. They were large, luminous, with a disconcertingly thick fringe of dark lashes. And she realized why ladies—of a certain type—fell for him.

"Got the cash?" There was a note of suppressed excitement in the Whippet's voice.

"Sure." Tex indicated her tan sport purse.

"Give us a look." The Whippet reached out a grasping, hairy hand.

Tex felt suddenly rather chilly and instinctively hugged her bag closer to her side, her alert mind working rapidly. Her purse held only a roll of stage money with an authentic yellow-back camouflaging it, a lipstick, powder compact, and her undersized gun. Her drawl was calm, collected when she answered: "Ah'm scared to take a chance—heah." She glanced around significantly. "If some gun-mob got hep to mah roll they'd lift mah leather."

The Whippet seemed to consider this, a queer, unreadable expression in his handsome eyes, then he said, "We'll beat it right over to the—kennels—so's—you can get back before the Border closes."

Tex followed them into the street and slid into the brilliant green roadster next to the Whippet. Cornita crowded in beside her.

Tex wasn't particularly elated over this arrangement. It cramped her style slightly, but at the present sitting she was rather helpless. She didn't want to tip her hand, so she grinned and proceeded to enjoy the ride. She was sharply aware of the surrounding country, of the vastness of the desert, of its jealous harboring of evil secrets, its endless waste—leading where?

As she moved her feet warily on the foot boards she felt the snaky eyes of Cornita creeping over her.

The Whippet was staring ahead at the narrow, sandy trail—trail that was obliterated as soon as the heavy tires had passed over it. And Tex thought with an inward shudder how easily a person could vanish in this cruelly mysterious country, leaving nothing behind but baffling silence over the impressionless sand.

As they sped further and further into the desert she began to wish she had heeded the chief's warning not to meddle in the Whippet's affairs. She couldn't hang anything on him and he might become a bit too rough for her to handle. She shrugged and dug her fingers into her bag. Well, she was in it now—

A high adobe wall loomed unexpectedly before them, a wall that was gloomy—crumbling, as old as Mexico itself and as impenetrable.

The Whippet pulled up in front of its single heavy wooden gate.

Cornita sprang down and Tex followed, stretching, swinging her arms, thankful to have her hands free to use again.

The Whippet pushed against the gate and a dozen growls

and yelps in as many different keys crashed against Tex's ears—sounds that trembled in discord, that were fraught with unnamed terror. She knew and loved dogs, but never before had she heard such poignantly human cries. She sent a lightning glance toward Cornita and noticed with a start that the dancer had gone suddenly white under her makeup. Her stubby hands were clenched spasmodically at her breast.

The gate swung in on tough rawhide hinges. The Whippet went through first, motioning for Tex and Cornita to follow.

He snapped out a word and at his familiar voice the screaming barks ceased abruptly.

Tex's apprehensive eyes shifted rapidly around the rather small enclosure. On two sides were twelve or more kennels built of stout wire about ten feet high, with wire roofs. No means of escape for the greyhounds except though the narrow wire entrances that were now padlocked.

On the side opposite the gate was a low stone house with a barred iron door and apparently no windows.

As the Whippet approached them the dogs cowered, crouching back on their haunches, stretching mouths over pointed fangs in silent snarls. Their eyes bloodshot, filled with a hate born of fear.

Tex's heart gave a queer little twist as she watched them, and her fingers itched to press the trigger of her .22, to plug the cruel two-legged beast who owned them. She laughed suddenly, a grating sound that caused Cornita and the Whippet to wheel and stare at her.

"This heah the layout Ah've got to pay twenty-five smacks for?" she asked.

"The fastest hounds in the country," snapped the Whippet.

"Ah'll take a squint at 'em," stated Tex, easing nearer the kennels. There was a half-formulated plan in her mind. She'd like to examine the mouths of those dogs. Dangerous business, she realized; foolish idea, too. What good would it do her? They were cowed, starving, snarling—but none of them was mad.

A sudden, blood-freezing scream tore into the enclosure, a scream that shivered through Tex like an ice-tipped blade, squeezing her heart, tightening her scalp. And a flash of light penetrated her slightly foggy thoughts, a revealing sense that had never failed her with its peculiar awareness of danger. She knew that cry, the cry of a mad dog she had once heard as a child. She had never forgotten its terrifying sound.

The hounds were moving restlessly around in their cages, emitting low, nervous growls.

Tex's eyes darted from them to the Whippet, whose face was expressionless—on to the dancer. She was staring at the little stone house, her black eyes wide, filled with panic.

"Dios Mio! Dios Mio!" she was muttering over and over. Her lips seemed to be dry, for she kept moistening them with the tip of her tongue.

"What you got in theah?" Tex jerked her head, indicating the stone house, while her strong fingers dug into her sport bag.

"The most valuable dogs in the country. The ones that bring me the biggest prices," answered the Whippet, and Tex thought she detected a gloating anticipation in his words.

She watched him pull a key from his pocket, and a slender thread of reasoning began to wind itself around her jerky nerves. She felt instinctively that what she was after was within the gruesome four walls of the stone house.

"Lead the parade, feller." She grinned at the Whippet, with

a grim twisting of her lips. "If Ah'm goin' to pony' up a pile of rocks, Ah got to see—the whole works."

The Whippet started toward the barred door of the house, unlocked it and pulled it toward him.

Tex was watching him closely. He took a pair of heavy gray leather gloves from his coat pocket and drew them over his hands.

Tex's heart was racing somewhere near her throat. The gloves were made of the same overweight gray leather as the one she had found in the bungalow of the last dog-bite victim.

She heard the sharp intake of breath as Cornita sucked it through her teeth, and something suddenly clicked in her a brain. But she must move carefully, play her cards cleverly. There was still a doubt, a fantastic idea to be logically explained.

That nerve-shattering screech came again, half human, half animal. A peculiar odor seeped out through the open door—like an unhealthy sewer, suffocating, nauseous. Tex's hand went to her nose as she peered over the Whippet's shoulder into the murky darkness before her. She could distinguish nothing save writhing shadows and gleaming eyes. It gave her a nightmarish sensation of unreality. She jerked hard at her everyday common sense, and looked at the Whippet with a smile that she forced through lips that felt strangely stiff. "Got a light? Ah can't see a damn thing." Her eyes slid involuntarily to his gloved hands.

He seemed to sense her unspoken question. "Racing hounds are vicious brutes. I gotter handle 'em with gloves," he explained with a defiant sort of laugh. He sent a veiled glance over his shoulder to Cornita, whom Tex noticed was hanging back with an odd look of anticipatory horror in her eyes.

"Turn on the glim," growled the Whippet.

Cornita moved slowly forward as if her feet were being pulled back by invisible strings, and pressed a switch near the entrance.

Tex gripped her purse a little tighter. She had a panicky feeling of present danger—of a trap ready to be sprung.

The black interior of the stone house was suddenly threaded with a dim yellow light that flickered weirdly over the half-dozen cages. In each cage there appeared to be a shallow, slimy pool and in the farthest corner from the germ-infested water crouched a small whippet, snapping, cringing, terrorized.

Tex's eyes stared longest at the corner cage—at the securely muzzled dog that ran frantically around his narrow cell, snapping at the bars with foam-flecked lips, glaring through eyes that were glazed with madness.

Tex's heart took a sudden, sickening plunge downward as she watched the crazed animal. Fear gripped her, shook her. Fear and horror and a fierce loathing for the savage who in some unknown manner had brought about this thing. He stood near the cage, fumbling with the padlock on the small door.

Tex tried to think of something to say, to remember what she had come for, to crow over her discovery, to reason away her blind Texan fury. But words refused to come. She couldn't utter them or even think them. Automatically, instinctively her hand flashed inside her bag and jerked out her small .22. "Now, damn you! Ah'll show you what we do to skunks like you— where Ah hail from!" She leveled as the Whippet wheeled to face her and lost the furtive movement behind her.

Cornita sprang on her like a tigress, clawing at her right arm, trying to knock the pistol from her hand, spoiling her aim, digging her thick, pointed nails into Tex's back—her neck and tearing the flesh. But Tex hadn't broken bronchos on her father's ranch for nothing. She was strong, lithe, canny. Her eyes never left the Whippet.

He had turned back and was holding the twisting, squirming animal by its strong leather collar. What was he doing with the strap that kept the muzzle in place? Tex's eyes dilated with a sudden horrifying knowledge.

Swiftly she lifted her right foot and gave a savage backward kick. The sharp heel of her low sport shoe caught Cornita in the knee. She cried out in startled pain and sat down unexpectedly, screaming at Tex, cursing her, her words spitting out like an infuriated cat's.

"You t'ink you tamn smart! You—Texas dick! You t'ink you fool us but we fool you instead—" She scrambled to her feet.

Tex felt the movement and eased a trifle to one side so that both the dancer and the Whippet were within her range of vision. Some of her clear reasoning came back to her. She would have to force a confession from the Whippet, bring proof to her chief that the moll buzzer was a murderer.

"We weel keel you the same way we—" the Mexican was raging when the Whippet stopped her with a warning gesture.

Tex laughed, an exultant little crow. Cornita had given their racket away. They were both killers! Using the dogs as blinds—or—? Still holding her pistol cocked in her right hand, she used her left to turn her purse upside down, emptying the contents on the slimy mud floor. Among the confusion of feminine necessities was a single gray leather glove. Swiftly, her eyes focused on Cornita and the Whippet. She swooped for the glove, straightened and threw it at the Whippet. It fell with a peculiar sharp smack at his feet.

He sprang back as if it had struck him. "God!" he muttered, his hold on the writhing, frothing dog relaxing for an instant. And in that instant the maddened dog jerked out of his grasp, the muzzle slipping from the foaming, snapping jaws.

The Whippet fought desperately to regain his hold on the collar, to yank the muzzle over the menacing teeth, to reach in his pocket for his gun, but his hands, covered with the thick gloves, were clumsy—useless. The dog gave its maniacal scream and lunged, sinking its poisoned fangs in the Whippet's arm.

"Quick! In my pocket—the—antitoxin," he yelled frantically to Cornita, but the dancer only stared at the crazed animal, unable to move, paralyzed with fear, stunned, helpless.

Tex's heart thumped against her lungs as she watched the deadly battle between man and beast. She felt suffocated. Her breath jerked through her dry lips in spasmodic gasps. Her brain whirled, speculated—planned. Her pistol was ready, but she didn't want to shoot the dog—yet. She wanted a confession first.

"You got—a rod—damn you—why don't you—kill—the mad—dog?" The Whippet was panting, fighting impotently against the snarling, foam-flecked lips.

Tex shifted her gaze hastily to the other cages. The dogs were growling, barking—running in excited circles. Then her eyes jerked back to the Whippet.

"Ah'll shoot—the pore hound—if you'll confess to those murders—in San Diego," she drawled at last.

The Whippet, his face sweat-smeared, streaked with blood-soaked froth, could only nod. His breath wheezed through gaping mouth. He staggered drunkenly.

"How did—you work it?" went on Tex evenly, although she had a strange quivering sensation in her stomach.

"Carried—dog—in—special—made—trunk," panted the Whippet. "For God's sake—shoot!"

The frenzied animal was plunging, lunging—tearing at his clothes. Driving him back—back— Then suddenly the Whippet unexpectedly slipped in the slime. He struggled to recover himself—only to be clawed down by the dog.

Too late Tex pulled the trigger. Too late the muffled cough of her .22, with its Maxim silencer, stiffened the thin, writhing body—stilled the snapping, crunching jaws.

The Whippet lay on his back, his leather-sheathed hands twitching, his wide, terrified eyes glazing, his throat gaping, spilling a river of crimson down his shirt—over the sticky mud floor.

There was a weird absence of sound, as if the stone house and those it imprisoned were frozen into silence.

Tex stared at the gruesome thing that had once been the Whippet, and forced unwilling feet to cross to it, herself to kneel and gingerly examine it. She noted with a pale, uncertain smile of triumph that the dog's teeth marks where the flesh hadn't been torn, were identical to those of the murder victims of two days ago—deep and pointed—with the exception of the left incisor—which was blunt—as if it had been broken off.

A stealthy shuffle pulled her up abruptly.

Cornita was closing the barred door from the outside—slyly padlocking it.

Tex sprang toward her and raised her pistol. "Open the door—or Ah'll shoot the works!" Her voice was cool—calm—yet she was trembling with a deadly conviction of impotence.

The Mexican only laughed, a laugh not unlike the cry of the mad dog—and spat through the bars. Dodging out of range, screaming, cursing in Spanish and English, her voice rose on a high note of hysteria. "If you get hungry—you tamn Texas dick—eat the dogs—" The last word broke off abruptly as if she were running and stumbled.

There came the sound of a frantically racing motor—and silence.

Tex shook the heavy iron door, tried unsuccessfully to squeeze her hand through the narrow openings between the bars, turned and stared at her nightmarish surroundings.

One of the dogs lifted its head and howled—a long, quivering moan.

Tex shuddered. God! Why hadn't she kept her eyes on Cornita?

HOW LONG SHE stood there—gripping those impervious bars, fighting the wild desire to laugh and sob and scream, she didn't know, but at last there was a faint, far-off rumble. She strained to see through the small openings—but could make out only part of the enclosure and the wooden gate that seemed to stare back at her gloatingly, challengingly.

Could it be Cornita returning? Someone else coming into the desert? Tex's heart thumped with doubtful hope.

The rumbling grew louder—louder! The unmistakable whir of a motor she had often heard—the even hum of the chief's swift little scout plane!

An interval of agonizing waiting, then voices, the Mexican's—thin, high-pitched, Jerry Gilbert's—coolly deliberate—relentless.

The gate was pushed violently in.

Cornita entered first, sullen, defiant—handcuffed. The chief came next, grim, prodding her with his blunt-nosed automatic, flashing his white smile when he saw Tex.

"Got yourself in a nice tight corner, eh, Tex?" he teased as he opened the iron door, although there was a hint of nervous concern in his tones.

"Hell!" was all she could jerk out.

"Thought you might need a little assistance," Jerry was explaining as Tex slid into the Whippet's green car, having tied the dancer securely in beside her. "So I flew down and nosed about until one of the Mexican police told me that you had gone toward the desert with Cornita and the Whippet." He stopped talking to adjust the strap on his helmet and smile at Tex. "I know you're curious to hear what Cornita told me about the Whippet's murder plot. He would sheik the rich widows first, promise to marry them and get them to sign over their fortunes, then smuggle a mad dog to their bungalows and—" He didn't finish but turned to the dancer. "Tell her the rest," he ordered.

The Mexican stared straight ahead, her shoulders sagging, her eyes expressionless, dull. Her voice, when she finally spoke, was flat. "It don't matter—now—that the—Whee-peet—ees gone. Wan day he find wan of hees hounds—ees mad. We want *mucho dinero*—so he t'ink of wan good plan. The first mad dog live only wan day—but Whee-peet put another dog in cage—so before he die he bite that wan—and that wan live t'ree days. He ees the wan Tex keel." She laughed suddenly, an insane, jarring sound. "*Mucho* funny. No wan t'ink murder!"

For a moment no one spoke. Nothing broke the vast stillness of the desert save the steady, even purr of the green roadster, then the chief took a cigarette from his pocket and tapped one end on his thumbnail. "I'll fly back to headquarters and you can motor in with—your prisoner."

He wheeled and started toward his plane, a graceful thing that was resting in the sand a short distance away, poised like an eager bird ready for instant flight.

Tex shifted into gear. "That'll be just—swell," she said with her characteristic grin, and was off.

The Silver Horseshoe

Tex of the Border Service trails a sinister sign

TEX HITCHED THE belt to her patched, whipcord breeches and eyed the silver insignia that was stamped on the racer's blanket. The gelding belonged to the Silver Horseshoe string; a string of six thoroughbreds that had been shipped in from some obscure farm west of the Rocky Mountains. Race horses owned by some unknown man; unnamed, obscure as his own stud farm, and represented by Tony Alvarado.

Tex instinctively mistrusted Tony. Not from anything she knew about him, but from some intangible warning that seemed to shiver through her whenever he was near.

She allowed her eyes to wander leisurely around the racer's box stall; to center with a slight inward start, on a mound of hay piled in the opposite corner from the manger that had not been in that position when she had left a little while ago to get her lunch.

Her eyes came back to the blanket and the silver horseshoe. Somehow that particular insignia interested her. It seemed to point a furtive finger at something hazy, ingenious, almost sinister. Something that she couldn't see—something that her keen, intuitive mind couldn't quite grasp.

She slid her right hand into the pocket of her breeches and eased a trifle nearer to the mound of hay—and paused—when a cautious squeak of leather made her turn toward the door of the stall. Her glance swept swiftly up from the man's stiffly new tan riding boots, to his tight, belted-in jacket; past his outthrust bluish chin, his thick, greedy lips, until her greenish-gold eyes stared into two pools of sooty black. Eyes that were unwinking, cold—unreadable.

Tex felt a little twinge of fear. Had he penetrated her disguise? Did he suspect who she was? What she was there for?

" 'Lo, Tony," she muttered in her slightly husky tones that might easily be taken for a boy's voice just changing.

Under the pretense of going over the gelding she studied Tony and detected a peculiar strained expression in his crafty face. Not in the bold, hard eyes, but something about the sensual lips. A tiny nerve that seemed to twitch uncontrollably at one corner. Tex had seen that same uncontrollable twitching of the mouth in criminals before and she had learned to watch for it. To her it meant fear of discovery—of what? Her eyes shifted to the silver horseshoe—and she wondered.

"Tam you! Tam you!" The guttural words of the Mexican thudded suddenly into her cogitations. She looked up at him then to see his low forehead puckered into a scowl of fury. "You tam lousy bum, you!"

Tex gave a slight start. For the moment she had entirely forgotten that she was now a boy, a new groom who had taken the place of the one preceding her—through the clever maneuvering of her chief.

"Why you don' get heem shod pronto?" he stormed. "You tam bum, you!"

"Furgot," mumbled Tex, lowering her head, not in sullen obsequiousness as Tony might have thought, but to hide the flush of anger that turned the gold of her eyes to a burning green flame.

Although she was staring down at the straw at her feet she sensed the indecision of Tony. He seemed to waver between

rage and some hidden dread. Her glance darted up as far as the Mexican's hands. They were big and hairy, with thick, cruel fingers that were now crushing spasmodically into his palms.

Tex shuffled hastily around to the racer's head. Tony had been known to slug his grooms if they were unlucky enough to rouse his temper. And she didn't care to be beaten up—just then. But she gave a satisfied inward chuckle. At least he still thought she was a boy.

She began fumbling with the gelding's halter, stroking his velvety muzzle—waiting for Tony to leave.

He did, finally, but not before he growled a parting injunction. "Get that horse shod tam pronto, savvy?"

"Yeah," answered Tex with just the right shade of servility sliding into her soft drawl. She watched his swaggering, gradually receding back. A back that seemed a little less aggressive—a little less sure of itself. Tony was evidently worried over the gelding's shoes. So was Tex.

She stared thoughtfully at the mound of hay in the corner, pondering, catching at an illusive thought that teased her clever reasoning—and was gone. Then her eyes widened in startled unbelief. Was she having a bad dream, or was the straw actually moving? She closed her eyes and snapped them open again. A foot was protruding from the hay. A flat, shoeless foot, with a hole in the toe of a black cotton sock.

Tex flashed her right hand inside her pocket and gripped the handle of her gun. "Come on out of theah!" Her low, throaty tones were commanding, threatening, albeit her knees felt a trifle weak.

There was a moment of frightened inactivity. The gelding moved restlessly, his small, pointed ears alert. Tex stood braced, ready—waiting. Then the hill of straw heaved suddenly upward and a tousled head shot into view.

"Gee, mister, don't shoot!" came in a thin, quavering voice.

Tex lowered her gun slightly in surprise as she appraised the boy who rose like a phantom before her. Red-haired, freckle-faced, snub-nosed, a large mouth filled with crooked teeth. But she noted particularly the boy's eyes. Not so much their dark blueness but the keenness of their expression—the look of maturity in their solemn depths, of wisdom beyond his years.

A smile twitched at the corners of her wide, humorous mouth and trickled down into her heart. "Gee yourself, son. What you playin' turkey in the straw for?" She pocketed her gun and the boy grinned.

He shook himself and plucked nervously at the hay that clung to his hair. His eyes darted swiftly around the stall, across the stable as far as he could see and back again to Tex. He raised a tentative, stubby-fingered hand and patted the gelding's neck. "You're the new groom, ain't you?" he asked unexpectedly in his high-pitched voice.

"Sure. One of 'em," answered Tex and turned her attention to the horse.

"So'm I," was his next startling disclosure.

Tex covered her surprise with a yawn. "Yeah?" She began to whistle—to rake the pungent hay from the mound in the corner and spread it over the floor of the stall. She was intent on her work but she felt that the boy was studying her with his unchildish eyes, and a chilly little doubt crept over her. Had he been sent by Tony to spy on her?

But his next words dispelled that doubt. "I stowed away on the box cars with the Silver Horseshoe string. They never got hep to me neither—till I landed here." He straightened his narrow shoulders with a motion of secret pride.

"What you do that fer?" Tex inquired casually.

He eyed her a trifle suspiciously and his answer gave her the impression that he was withholding some of the truth. "On'y way I could get to come to the races." He shot out his small square chin and looked at her unblinkingly—defiantly. "They wouldn't let me be a jockey, 'cause I'm too young. Huh, I know more 'bout ridin' than that bum Greaser?"

"Yeah?" said Tex, feigning indifference. She smoothed the blanket on the gelding's back, watching the boy closely as he kicked at the straw with one stockinged foot, his alert blue eyes roving, seeking. He seemed expectantly fearful—of what—Tony? She wondered. "What racin' mule you wet-nursin'?" she asked.

"Sun-maid." He pointed a grimy, blunt finger at the right-hand adjoining stall.

Tex wanted to ask him why he had hidden in her stall—to ask him a dozen other questions, but she didn't. She must move slowly, cautiously, for, although she understood and liked youngsters and they usually were eager to answer her apparently guileless quizzing, she felt, instinctively, that this particular boy was too wary, too distrustful, to be approached in the usual method. And would only talk when his confidence was placed—and proven.

The chief, relying upon her ever-ready, clever wit, her sane deducing powers, had put her on the case. And it was a case that had been upsetting the traditions of the racing game at Tia Juana; mystifying the track superintendents and race-horse owners. A case that was mysterious, baffling—intangible.

To Tex, it was more than coincidence that three well-known jockeys, a week apart, had been kicked to death just before they were to ride the heavily staked favorites, and an unknown rider put up; a rider who always lost—to one of the Silver Horseshoe string. Her mind swung around to Lome, the ablest jockey in the game, who was to ride tomorrow—Best-bet, a three-year-old from the Arrowhead stables. A thoroughbred that had never been beaten. Would anything happen to Lome? Tex gave an involuntary shiver.

"Cheese!" The hissing whisper stabbed sharply into Tex's apprehensions, snapping her to attention.

The boy was pulling at her sweater sleeve. She looked down into the earnest freckled face. "Yeah?" Her soft drawl invited confidence.

The boy hesitated, then he blurted as if wanting to rid himself of some gnawing secret. "I hate that Greaser! He's a lotta hooey."

"Yeah?" Tex encouraged.

"Yeah—him 'n' my stepfather both. Huh, I know things 'bout

'em—" He stopped short, his eyes growing suddenly round with fear as they stared past Tex to the door of the stall.

Tex followed his gaze, her own eyes narrowing, her shoulders hunching a little forward.

Tony stamped into the stall. A raging Tony with a cruel twist to his mouth, a venomous expression in his dark eyes.

Tex didn't care particularly for the look he shot at her and she fussed clumsily with the halter rope before she could untie it. She started to lead the gelding past him, but he barred her way, his attitude one of menace, distrust.

"Goin' to get this heah cayuse shod now," she volunteered, easing a bit nearer the wooden entrance.

Tony glowered at her, his great, hairy paws clenching into fists. "Why in hell didn' you do it before?"

Tex's smile stiffened, but held, and she let her lids droop over her eyes in an assumption of servility.

Tony appeared to be mulling something over within the confines of his thick skull; then unexpectedly he turned on the boy. "What in hell you doin' here?"

The boy edged a little closer to Tex, as if seeking her uncertain protection, although his voice was staunch enough when he answered, "Just come to see this horse." He reached out one of his grubby little hands and stroked the thoroughbred's glistening neck.

A peculiar change came over Tony. A change that had an electrifying effect on Tex as she covertly watched him. Could it be that he feared this youngster? A grim smile flashed across the firm lips of Tex—and was gone. Tony, like the coyote, was a coward; only striking in the dark. Still, fear, in the bullying type, she realized, was dangerous—leading to crime—even— murder. She shivered, and decided she wouldn't care to meet

Tony in the shrouded byways of the Mexican borderland.

"You look after your own horse," Tony's voice growled.

"Goin' to," the boy was mumbling, an odd mixture of submissiveness and satisfaction edging into his treble tones. But he didn't leave immediately; instead he poked around in the straw with his stockinged feet.

Tex and Tony watched him in silence. Tony, scowling, hesitating. Tex, with curiosity, and admiration for the youngster's bold unconcern. Finally she asked, "What you lookin' fer?"

"M' shoes. Hid 'em here some place," the boy answered and went on with his search.

Out of the tail of her eye, Tex saw Tony go rigid; heard the hissing intake of his breath and wondered why the mention of shoes always seemed to startle him out of his usual bulldozing.

She gave her characteristic shrug. A slight, upward motion of her slim shoulders that, in her, was the outward sign of some arresting thought pulling at her clever mind—pointing a wavering finger at the hazy outlines of one of her hunches. Fantastic, perhaps, but one she was always ready to follow.

Tony stayed until the boy had found his shoes, then with a grunt he stamped out of the stall.

Tex watched him go with an inward sigh of relief, and turned back to the boy.

He was sitting on the floor, pulling on a pair of scuffed shoes. He grinned up at her, but it was a wise, secretive sort of a grin. A grin that didn't quite match Tex's idea of boyhood.

She stared at him for a moment without speaking, then, "What else you huntin' fer?" The question came unexpectedly, taking the boy off his guard as she had expected that it would.

His face suddenly sobered—became sullen. His bright blue

eyes slid from her to his shoes, and remained there. "Nothin'."
His thin, childish voice sounded oddly old and flat and his
stubby little fingers fumbled with the knotted laces of his boots.

Tex's desire was to question him further, but some warning
within her held her back—whispered to her to wait. The set
of his small, square jaw denoted a stubbornness that would be
difficult to swerve, but she had the feeling that when he was
ready to confide in her he would.

She also knew in some intuitive way that this boy's playtime
had been crushed out of him. He gave the impression of a boy
who had existed in an environment of harsh realities. Realities
that were sordid, unchildlike—cruel. Studying him, Tex's heart
felt suddenly tight and heavy. What was the dark shadow that
crouched back of his too-brilliant blue eyes?

Tex shuffled forward, leading the gelding. "S'long," she
drawled and left him sitting there—in the straw, nervously
pulling at the laces of his shoes.

With assumed unconcern she slouched past the long line of
box stalls, into the paddock, across the paddock, toward the
blacksmith shop. She shrugged impatiently and wished that
she could talk to her chief, glean some of his deeper knowledge—understanding, but she didn't dare risk a long-distance
phone call. It was too early in the game—besides grooms were
watched suspiciously before the big races.

She looked up suddenly to encounter the weazened little face
of the jockey Lome. He regarded her seriously for an instant,
then he smiled, a tentative, rather sad smile, Tex thought, as
she answered it with her own good-natured grin.

Lome spoke first. "One of the Silver Horseshoe string?" He
nodded toward the gelding.

"Yeah. Hear you're aimin' to win the sweepstakes with Best-bet tomorrer," Tex rejoined, watching to see if there was any change of expression in the jockey's sober face; there was none. He merely stared at her, his voice even, almost toneless, as he answered, "Best-bet'll win all right—if I ride." He shifted his gaze once more to the gelding.

A cold shiver trickled along Tex's spine. "Thought you was up?" Her husky voice implied a question.

Lome nodded slowly, his eyes shifting from the thoroughbred's pointed ears to his muzzle, his deep chest, his clean forelegs; up again to his head, along his back and almost fearfully to his hind legs—and hoofs. When he finally spoke, his words gave Tex the impression of one who is speaking his thoughts aloud. Thoughts that worried him—frightened him. "Sure. I'm up, but—" He raised his eyes swiftly and gave her a searching stare. A stare that stabbed her suddenly with an uneasy sense of dread.

He finished his sentence then, speaking rapidly. "Best-bet's won some of the biggest races in the country—but—that was before the Silver Horseshoe blew into the Tia Juana track." His eyes slid once more to the gelding. He nodded, mumbled something Tex couldn't hear, and hurried on his way.

Tex stared after him, her mind filled with conflicting emotions, confused impressions. She gave an involuntary shudder. Lome feared the Silver Horseshoe. Was he afraid that he, too, would be kicked to death before the race tomorrow?

IT WAS DUSK before she led the gelding back to the stables. Dusk, silent—brooding dusk, that settled into a motionless waiting—watching, like a skulking wolf, for the closing of the

Border—for the restless seekers of thrills to weave their zigzag paths over the Line to San Diego.

Tex felt a little nervous chill shoot through her. A chill of impending danger; of something unknown—unnamed. Something grimly hidden. The rope in her hand grew suddenly taut, sending a slight shock down her arm. She looked up at the racer. His head was thrown back, his ears pricked forward. His sensitive nostrils quivered. He planted his feet and stopped dead at the entrance of his stall and gave a short, sharp snort. A sound that Tex had often heard on her father's ranch back in Texas. The warning cry that a horse gives when he senses danger.

Quickly she shifted the halter rope to her left hand, flashed her right hand into her pocket and gripped the butt of her .22. She looked into the stall but could distinguish nothing unusual in the dim light. Her eyes searched the four corners, the manger, the straw bedding on the floor. Everything apparently was as it should be, yet something was wrong. The gelding had sensed it and she, understanding and loving horses, trusted a good deal to their unconsciously keen guidance.

Patiently she urged the thoroughbred into his stall, looped the halter rope through the manger, and ventured into the right-hand stall adjoining, where Sun-maid was securely tied. She glanced hastily around, but the boy had not returned. Slowly she retraced her steps and tried to settle herself comfortably on her lumpy straw bed.

She closed her eyes but sleep refused to come. Her seething thoughts kept her wide-awake; her brain alert. Somehow the absence of the boy worried her. His glowing blue eyes kept intruding between her and rest. There was something about the kid that tugged at her heart. She sighed, stretched, rolled over; endeavoring to push the disturbing thoughts from her mind. Why should she fret over the boy? He was probably all right. He knew how to take care of himself. But did he? After all he was only a kid. He seemed so valiant—so alone. And Tony was so huge, so brutal!

Tex jerked suddenly to her feet. If the boy was trailing Tony, then she should be trailing the boy.

Mustering a calmness she didn't feel, she ambled along from stall to stall, her strong, capable hands hidden within the pockets of her breeches, casually asking the grooms if they had seen the boy.

They answered sleepily, indifferently, that they hadn't. A growing fear seeped into her heart; rage gripped her, shook her. If Tony harmed that kid! Her mouth set in a grim, straight line.

She moved on to the last stall, that was a little apart from the others. Best-bet's stall. She hesitated before the door, her natural sense of detail cognizant of the fact that the door was bolted from the outside, as all box-stall gates are. However, this fact only registered vaguely in her mind. Probably Lome had left for a few minutes.

She stared in at the restive racer, undecided. Save for the horse the stall was empty, yet, another detail recorded itself on her mind, more forcibly this time; when a groom leaves his horse alone he usually ties him. Best-bet was loose backed into the farther corner, facing Tex; quivering, his ears flattened against his head, his lips drawn back over his teeth.

Watching him, the warm human blood of Tex turned to ice. Knowing horses as she did, she was certain that something was wrong here. She controlled the excited quaver in her voice and spoke quietly to the thoroughbred.

He pricked his ears, then flattened them again. She drew back the bolt and softly opened the door with her left hand. Her right one she kept inside her pocket.

She pulled the door to after her. "Easy, boy, easy," she crooned as she advanced slowly toward him.

He eyed her hopefully, suspiciously, cocking first one ear, then the other, then both—and flattened them back again.

Then something pulled her around. Not a motion, not a sound; something strange, unnatural. Tex backed against the manger, her eyes on the door. No one was there—nothing. Quickly her eyes slid around the stall, to focus with a start on a dark object that looked like some fixed shadow crouching in the dimmest corner. She edged nearer to it, panic pulling her back, necessity urging her forward. Just for an instant she hesitated, then stooping swiftly she brushed aside some of the straw that was clinging to the body—and drew back with a jerk. Her fingers felt sticky. She looked at them. They were red—red with fresh blood. A shaft of icy fear shivered through her. God! Could it be the boy? She gritted her teeth. If that youngster was hurt, she'd take whoever did it for a ride! A long, returnless ride!

She bent over again, using one hand, forcing herself to touch carefully the gruesomely twisted limbs. With agitated fingers and her heart racing somewhere between her left lung and her throat, she turned the body slightly toward her.

Lome stared up at her—with the glazed stare of death. Death that had come swiftly—violently. The right side of his head was crushed in. Blood was already drying in large clots on his face, his neck, and still dripping down over his shoulder.

Tex's knees felt suddenly weak as she gazed at the thing that had once been the famous jockey. There was a taste of salt in her mouth; a huge hand seemed to be wrenching at her stomach. She closed her eyes an instant and fought the overwhelming nausea that seized her. She jerked hard at her swaying thoughts—steadied them—stood them up in order—and opened her eyes. Gradually their expression changed from horror to pity, blazed into fury; resolution to track down this man, beast—thing—whatever it was that had trampled out the life of Lome in such a hideous fashion.

She knelt down beside him, compelling herself to examine the ghastly, beaten-in head more closely. The wound was in the shape of a horseshoe, with bits of hay and dirt adhering to the drying blood. In the center of the U-shaped scar was a deep, narrow hole that looked as if a nail from the shoe had been loosened and driven in by the force of the blow.

Quietly she turned to the racer, easing up to him with outstretched hand, coaxing him, crooning to him. He jerked his head back, flattening his ears and giving a snort of fear. Tex stopped, still talking to him in her soft drawl; reached in one of her pockets and drew out a lump of sugar. The horse watched her suspiciously, working his ears back and forth. She edged nearer. Warily he sniffed at her hand and finally nosed the sugar on to the floor. She stroked his velvety muzzle, patted his shining neck, then ran her fingers carefully along his fore legs, his hind legs.

He lifted them in turn as she gave each a slight pressure just above the ankle, taking a swift, sure survey of the iron shoes that fitted his hoofs. She found what she expected. On the right hind shoe a nail extended a little beyond the iron rim.

She bent nearer and inspected it more closely. On the head of the nail was a small brown stain—that might have been dirt—or dried blood.

Outwardly calm, almost indifferent, she slouched across the stall, pushed the door open a little wider with her left hand and eased through. Her eyes slid quickly around the stable, but there was no one—nothing—only the faint glow of electric lights that pointed feeble fingers to the line of box stalls that housed the racers; a soft crunching sound as the horses nosed their mangers; occasionally the sharp stamping of hoofs; spasmodic snores from the grooms as they shifted uneasily in their lumpy beds of straw, while each guarded his particular racer.

She slipped by them all noiselessly, a swift, furtive shadow.

ACROSS THE PADDOCK Tex ran, and over the short plank bridge toward Old Town. An Old Town that was abandoned, slinking, at this hour of the night. Every now and then she glanced nervously over her shoulder. Was she being followed? She strained her eyes, trying to penetrate the darkness. Shadows stretched back of her. Shadows and—silence. If she were caught by these hidden instigators of crime, her life wouldn't be worth that! Mentally she snapped her fingers—and shivered. She had never been afraid to die—but—hell—being stabbed in the back wasn't her idea of having a good time. She made a wry face and hurried on.

At the end of the street where the Foreign Club stood stark and lonely, Tex turned abruptly to the right, on to a narrow back street, unpaved, deserted. She was following one of her rational hunches. A hunch that beckoned her to Tony Alvarado's squalid living quarters. A small, squat adobe; crumbling, worm-eaten; cowering like some evil old witch behind an enveloping wall of spiny cacti.

Noiselessly she crept around the scraggly fence, pausing, listening, groping for the concealed opening that she knew led into an arid, weed-grown patio. At last she found it and crawled through. A low, black object loomed before her; the black shadow of the crouching adobe.

She came erect with a jerk of fright. A stealthy rustle had slithered unexpectedly into the stillness. She tensed, listening, waiting—afraid to use her flashlight. Then an anguished moan stirred the hair on her scalp. It quivered through the dark, silent night like an infernal spirit, then ceased abruptly as if some giant hand had smothered it into choking silence.

Tex's feet felt suddenly heavy, wooden; her arms useless; her thoughts confused. She stood facing the cloudy menace of the adobe, her back to the opening she had just come through. Her fingers curled around her gun as she pulled it slowly from her pocket, but even the feel of its cool, hard handle didn't shake the queer unreality that seemed to hold her.

Stillness came again. Stillness that filled her with every imaginable horror. "Gawd!" she muttered through stiff, dry lips—and—"Gawd!" again when a groan again pierced her mental fog; an intensely human groan that came from somewhere near at hand. A groan that held a startlingly familiar treble note; a groan that caused her breath to catch in her throat; her heart to take a sickening downward plunge.

Her brain was clicking clearly now, had shot back to normal; still she hesitated, gripping her .22, advancing warily. It might be a trick to throw her off her guard. She eased cautiously along the hedge of cacti, shuffling her feet over the rotting, uneven stones of the patio until finally the exploring toe of her boot struck something soft and yielding.

Using her electric-torch was risky business, but she had to know—had to be sure. The white, revealing arc flashed for an instant over the huddled form of the boy; over his pale, pinched features; the cruel, straining gag in his mouth; his bound wrists and ankles.

Tex switched off the light and pocketed the torch, but not before she had read the message in the boy's eyes; wise, brave eyes that looked up at her with a cool, eager stare in their brilliant blue depths.

With her vigilance centered on the adobe and the surrounding shadows, every faculty alert for the least sound or movement, Tex bent swiftly over the boy and jerked off the gag with her left hand.

"Got a knife?" She spilled the words out of the corner of her mouth in a sibilant whisper.

The boy gulped two or three times before he could manage a squeaky, "Sure—pants'—pocket," and as Tex searched frantically, "Cheese—I'm—glad—you come!"

Tex's throat felt suddenly tight. "Yeah," was all she could jerk out.

She extracted the knife from a tangle of nails, string, chewing-gum. Snapped open the strong, sharp blade and slashed at the heavy cords that bound him, then helped him to a sitting position.

Stiffly, painfully he stretched his arms, his legs, and Tex was conscious of the little click of his teeth as they ground together in his effort to keep from crying out.

"Tony in theah?" she whispered.

"Sure."

"Anybody with him?"

"Yep, m' stepfather. The big stiff!" gritted the boy, crawling weakly to his feet. He swayed against Tex and she put her left arm around his shoulders to steady him.

"Anybody else?" she asked.

"Nope, on'y the two of 'em."

"Now, ain't that just—swell?" A little gurgle of relief slid into Tex's guarded tones. Two. Hell! That was easy—provided she saw them first; she pressed her fingers into his arm—to hold his attention. "What Ah'm itchin' to know is, how did you get heah?" she went on.

"I was trailin' the big cheese 'n' he caught me," was the boy's simple answer.

"Ah'm still curious, son, what made you trail Tony?" Tex felt the boy's hesitancy and imagined that he was trying to penetrate the gloom with his searching eyes; trying to see her face—make out her game, and she decided suddenly to trust him; to show him all her cards—face up. Her voice sank to a confidential murmur, "Listen, son, do you know who Ah am?"

"Nope."

"Well, son, I'm a Secret Service operator an' I got business down here on the Border."

"Cheese!"

She felt that he was staring up into her face and unconsciously she smiled at him in the darkness, then she tautened—a faint, menacing rustle stole into the silent patio, followed again by the eerie wail—prolonged—blood-chilling.

"Gawd! What's that?" Somehow Tex was glad that the boy was with her.

"Aw—that ain't nothin'. They're just tryin' to scare me, but I ain't no baby." His whisper was plucky enough, although Tex could feel an uncontrollable trembling shake him as he pressed closer to her side.

Then Tex came to one of her lightning decisions. "Better spill all you know, son, an' spill it quick," she urged, and as the boy seemed to hesitate, "so they want to scare you?"

"Sure," he whispered earnestly. "My stepfather did scare me—first—when I was little—to keep my trap shut—after—" He stopped short as if the memory hurt him, then went on doggedly, "After—I seen 'im kill my—mother." The last word ended in a dry little sob and Tex couldn't speak for a moment; when she did her voice had a rough edge to it—sounded uneven in her own ears.

"Killed—your mother?"

"Uh-huh. He—he—wanted to get hold of all her horses."

"M'n. An' now your steppah owns the Silver Horseshoe string."

"Sure."

"Listen, son, Ah'm trailin' Tony—" The boy interrupted eagerly, his voice shaking with excitement. "Gosh, mister—then you, too, seen 'im hide it in your stall, so's he'd have it handy—huh?"

Tex didn't know just what "it" was, but she was going to find out. "Yeah, but somebody must've cribbed it again, because when Ah looked—it was gone!"

"Cheese! Then how're we goin' to prove they done it?" His treble voice was shaky with disappointment.

Suddenly someone laughed. A cruel, deep-throated laugh.

Tex stiffened. Then a blinding circle from a flashlight brought her into bold relief against the black shadows. Her arm tightened about the youngster's shoulders as she blinked in the unexpected glare. The fingers of her right hand dug a little harder into her pistol. She moistened her dry lips and forced them into a semblance of her gamin-like grin. "Reckon you don't know it, Tony, but Ah cain shoot just as straight with mah eyes shut," she drawled, endeavoring to hide the depressing sense of failure that engulfed her. Failure and chagrin and fear. Inwardly she cursed her stupidity; her lack of rigid vigilance. Engrossed in the boy's story, she had failed to hear the stalking of the Mexican.

"You too slow. I keel you first—like I keel all the jockeys." Tony was gloating and he laughed again, the light jumping fantastically up and down as his huge frame shook the hairy left hand that held it. Then he lunged at her, swinging something that seemed to be heavy in his right hand.

"Cheese! That's *it!*" screamed the boy and ducked—trying frantically to pull Tex down with him.

But she fired first—square into the center of the blinding light—a spurt of flame, a soft, unobtrusive little pop. Then the thud of a falling body—darkness—silence.

Tex pulled her own flash out of her pocket and turned it on Tony. He was sprawled face down at her feet, the broad, strong handle of an axe clutched in his right hand. She bent nearer and examined it curiously. On one end an ordinary iron horseshoe was securely fastened, and in the center of the U a long nail protruded.

She stared at it with wonder at its ingenuity—horror at its brutality, then into the small patch of light from her torch, a large black boot thrust itself. Startled, Tex jerked up her gun and flash simultaneously.

A man was glaring at her. A short, stocky man, with heavy shoulders and thick, red features. There was a gun in his hand. A menacing, snub-nosed automatic.

For an instant, as she stared into his ape-like face, terror shook her, then her eyes darted to a crawling shadow back of him, and surprise and hope pulled at her unsteady nerves. "Attaboy!" she called unexpectedly, and, as if answering her signal, the boy wound his thin arms around the man's legs, throwing him forward.

There was a sharp explosion, a flash of fire as the automatic was torn from his hand when he clawed desperately to free himself.

"Swell work, son," crowed Tex, edging nearer the man. "Stick out your mitts, bo," she urged him.

Slowly he stretched his hands out in front of him. "Say, you," he growled, "that's my kid. I'll get you jailed for kidnaping him."

Tex grinned; not a particularly friendly grin, "Zat so?" Then she addressed the boy, "Listen, son, theah's a sweet pair of steel bracelets in mah pocket. Put 'em on your pah."

The boy obeyed with alacrity, smiling broadly, showing all his crooked teeth. "Gosh," he exclaimed, snapping on the handcuffs, "I'd like to be a dick!"

Tex laughed. "That's easy. Ah'll just speak to the chief about you."

The boy's bright blue eyes grew round with almost poignant anticipation, "Will you? Cheese! You're great!"

"Yeah," muttered Tex.

Tijuana Red

"TIJUANA RED," THEY called her, down on the Mexican border, just across the line from San Diego. A bit of jetsam tossed up out of the stormy sea of nowhere, drifting in on its muddy stream to sink in squalid splendor in a small dark room over one of the numerous cantinas in the filthy settlement of Old Town.

About five feet in height and slenderly round. Her features, small and pointed. Her eyes, deep set and russet in color with amber glints. Her hair, as fine in texture as a baby's, clinging to her small well shaped head in soft Titian curls. Her skin, of that unblemished pallor that occasionally goes with red hair. Of indifferent Swedish parentage. No one knew her real name, nor cared. Education, she had none, but possessed a rare uncultured philosophy.

During the racing season she followed the track at Tijuana, getting tips from the bar-tenders, bookies and sometimes from the jockies themselves, making extra pocket money. Everybody liked her. She was a good sport and always played fair. The first to help a friend in need, and, contrary to the old adage of red hair, never lost her temper. Perhaps she had none to lose.

"She's too Swedish," as one of her inebriated buddies expressed it.

Unlike the heavy red wine of Mexico, she sparkled and one could always find her in any one of the saloons, with an ever ready smile turning up the corners of her provocative rouged lips, and her characteristic, "How's tricks?" which was accompanied by a negligent salute. After which she would swagger to the bar with some slightly intoxicated, or otherwise pleasure bent gentleman in tow, place one foot on the brass rail, light a cigarette and blithely call for, "Whiskey straight."

Tijuana Red was a privileged character, for unlike the other derelicts of the border, she came and went as she chose and was extremely particular to whom she bestowed the favor of sharing her room for the night. To the casual outsider she was just one of the girls, and albeit she was friendly with them all and shared everything she had with them, from men to money and clothes, her thoughts she jealously kept to herself.

Now, Red, her foot on the rail, her right hand on her hip, her left elbow on the bar, her left hand supporting her head, a half finished cigarette dangling loosely from the corner of her mouth, called in her high pitched strident voice, "Whiskey straight, you know me, Danny." Then turning from her fat, middle aged partner who leered in her face and pawed her with maudlin affection, leaned confidentially to the bar-tender and whispered, "Make it plain gingerale, Danny, I'm gar-gar enough as 'tis."

With a knowing wink, Danny set two small glasses filled with a golden brown liquid side by side on the bar.

Red raised her glass to her lips. "Here's to Daddy's crossword puzzle." She laughed and downed hers in one gulp.

Her fat friend reached for his drink with an unsteady hand and lifted it shakily as far as his double chin. "Whosh cross words?" he giggled drunkenly.

"Thash a good 'un," appreciated Red, raising her knee playfully and giving him a gentle push with the sole of her foot. Her well aimed kick landed somewhere in the vicinity of the

gentleman's embonpoint. He grunted, tottered, lost his equilibrium all together and eased to a sitting position on the brass rail.

With a laugh and shrug Tijuana Red popped a wad of chewing gum in her cheek and sauntered with her peculiarly swaying motion to the swinging doors, through them and out into the dark balmy night. With her hands thrust in the pockets of her jade silk sweater she swaggered jauntily along the dimly lighted main street on its rough board walk, past the Gringo hot dog man who hailed her with a flourish of his pancake turner, past the dirty little Mexican curio store and past the cantinas from which a jumble of jazz smote the air with discordant sound.

In the doorway of the last saloon on the corner just before you turn sharply to the right to cross the rickety bridge to Tijuana, lounged a woman inclined toward obesity. She was wrapped in the flamboyant costume of the dance halls. Her dark muddy complexion, showing the Mexican strain, was smeared with rouge and dead white powder and her short hair, black at the roots, was bleached a bright straw color.

Catching sight of Tijuana Red she waved her cigarette. " 'Lo, Red, where yuh rompin' to?"

" 'Lo, Rose, just goin' ter give the Casino the double oo. Nothin' don' here ternight."

"Gawd, but yuh got easy pickins. I gotter stick around this dump or I'll lose muh job. Hellava life, this is!" She spat viciously.

Red laughed and shrugged. "S'long."

"If yuh lamp Tony, tell'um his bad momo's cravin' his company." Rose laughed raucously and turned back into the cantina.

"Poor Rose," muttered Red, thinking of Tony, the Mexican half breed, as handsome and perfect physically as a bronze statue, and as evil as the worse half of both races. The mixture of Indian and Mexican blood that ran riot in his veins was bad medicine. For three years he and Rose had lived together in a dirty little hovel on one of the crooked back streets of Old Town. When first Rose had left her poor but respectable home, her fat good-for-nothing father, her brow-beaten, worn-out mother and ten squalling sisters and brothers, she had been considered rather a beauty. Midnight hair and large slumberous black eyes that could smolder suddenly into a flame of passionate love or passionate jealousy as the case might be, and for Tony they had flamed alternately. The past year he had strayed more and more, and when he was with her he abused her, but the more he beat her the more she worshipped him, giving him all of the money that she earned at the cantina, painting her face and bleaching her hair to try to keep him because he had fallen for a pale-faced, golden-haired Gringo.

Tony had recently secured for himself the dignified position of bar-tender, at the Casino at Tijuana. It gave him the opportunity for which he was seeking; the opportunity of serving drinks to the Americanos, and especially to the pretty Americano ladies. There was one in particular—Betty Southerland— they called her—she had a husband—but—bah—what did he care for husbands? Hadn't she openly flirted with him, Tony? All this, Tony being in a confidentially inebriated mood one night had confided to Red.

"Poor Rose." So ruminated Tijuana Red as she neared the unlighted bridge that led to the Casino.

Half way across it she stumbled over a huddled form. "Yeasus!" she exclaimed, stooping and feeling the body with sensitive trained fingers. "It's a lady, by Gar." She took a box of matches out of her pocket and struck one, holding it close to the girl's face. She looked long at the closed eyes, flushed cheeks and partly open mouth. "Pretty—pretty—drunk," she finally concluded.

"Leave 'er lay," came a hoarse whisper from the darkness.

" 'Lo, Tony, kinder had a hunch you was in on this," answered Red, straightening.

"I can't help it if the lady demands of me to serve her too much drinks." Tony emerged suddenly from the shadows and stooping swiftly picked the unconscious girl up in his arms. "I'll take care of 'er."

Tijuana Red caught him by the sleeve. "No yuh won't, yuh'll take the Jane straight ter my room an' *I'll* take care of 'er, see?"

He lowered at her. "You mind your tarn business! She's mine."

"I'll mind your tarn business an' make it my tarn business to notify the Gringo police about that little tarn business of yours that happened to the Gringo sailor las' week, get me?"

Tony hesitated and spat out a few choice Mexican swear words.

"Get a wiggle on," hissed Red, "the skirt needs attention."

He got, walking sullenly beside her, carrying the unconscious girl gingerly, as if she were a china doll.

In the dingy, poorly lighted hall back of the cantina where Red lived, they encountered Danny. He grinned knowingly at sight of the limp form. "Passed out?" He inquired with a wink.

Red nodded. "Sure. Cold."

Tony said nothing but his brows were drawn together in an ugly scowl.

"Now, beat ut, yuh dirty half-breed," spat Red when the girl had been dumped in a rumpled heap on the bed.

"I'll get you—and her—too," he snarled.

Red took a threatening step forward. "Get ter hell out—an' don' ferget the Gringo sailor!"

Tony drew his lips back from his clenched teeth in impotent rage and shaking his fist in her face strode out, slamming the door with a bang that shook the whole building.

Tijuana Red laughed and turned to the girl, who was now moaning in a drunken stupor.

"Poor Jane," muttered Red compassionately kneeling beside her. Suddenly she sprang up. "The damn skunk, he's doctored his fire-water with ether," and as the girl moved her lips feebly, "you're sure goin' ter be some poisoned pup. Yeasus!" And Red administered to the best of her knowledge.

The girl sat up with a groan and stared blearily at the red-headed phantom who regarded her with such a sympathetic smile.

"How'd you get in?" she mumbled.

Red laughed. "It don' take no crossword puzzle ter answer that. I roost here. Now, lie down, dearie, I won't let nobody bother yuh." Red put a soothing hand on her brow.

The girl sank back on the pillow with a sigh. "Where am I? My God, my head's splitting!"

Red drew up a chair and sat down.

"Ugh," groaned the girl.

"Yeasus, kid, I didn' mean ter joggle the bed," apologized Red.

The girl stared stonily at the ceiling. "Where am I, and who are you?" She asked again.

"You're at a dirty little dump called Old Town, right acrost from Tijuana."

"Oh." The girl began to whimper, the maudlin tears trickling down her cheeks. "My b-brain's all be-befuddled. I c-can't remember, b-but Tijuana sounds ff-familiar. My God, my head's splitting!"

Red nodded wisely. "Yeh, I know, dearie, I been there myself. Many's the hangover I been wet-nurse ter. Yeasus!" She chuckled reminiscently.

The girl made a weak attempt to rise. "I must go," she muttered.

"Where?" inquired Red, steadying her.

"Home." She slumped weakly against Red.

"Where's—home?"

"Coronado. We've only been there a month. Oh, I must—get home. My husband would kill me if he knew!" She began to weep softly on Red's shoulder.

Red put her arms around her and petted her and cooed to her as if she were a child. "There, there, dearie, don' yuh worry. Yuh'll be all jake in the morning."

The girl sat up with a jerk. "In the morning!" She fairly screamed. "Those old tabbies would find it out and tell my husband. I must—go—now!" She rose resolutely, biting hard on her under lips.

Red gazed at her helplessly. "Sorry, kid, but yuh can't. It's too late."

"Too late? What do you mean?"

"The boarder closes at twelve. It's after one now."

"But I've got to—don't you see—I've just got to! It would be too awful to stay away all night! Dick would never forgive me. He'd suspect—the—worst—after those cats finished with me!" She flung out her hands in desperate entreaty.

"Mud slingers—huh?"

The girl nodded miserably.

Tijuana Red chewed her gum thoughtfully. "Yeasus," she said at last, "Yeasus, kid, I'm sorry fer yuh but—it can't be done. They're awful strict an' anyway—"

The girl swayed and slid silently to the floor.

"An' anyway, yuh couldn't make the grade, dearie," Red finished. Gently she undressed the girl and put her to bed, then she sent for some ice water.

When she went to the door to take the pitcher from the boy a man lurched toward her. "'Lo sweet patootie," he said with a leer, and pushing past the boy he placed one unsteady foot across the threshhold.

"Can't come in ternight, Joe," said Red firmly.

He stopped short in amazement. "S'matter? Gettin' hellish choosey allava sudden," he sneered.

Red laughed good naturedly. "Sorry, Joe, but I already got a friend—a sick-lady friend."

"Shick lady fren'—hah, thash a good one—shome damn fool beat me to it, s'ats all." He drew himself up with drunken dignity and weaved his uncertain way down the hall.

With her characteristic shrug Red closed the door and locked it.

THE FIRST GRAY fingers of dawn crept through the dusty, fly-specked window and caressed the bright bent head of Tijuana Red as she sat nodding in the only chair the small bed room afforded. "Yeasus!" She got stiffly to her feet and stretched her aching body. "One hellava night!"

The girl on the bed stirred and opened her eyes. "You've been awfully good to—to—take care of me," she murmured.

"Aw, 'tain't nothin'."

The girl smiled a bit wryly. "Was I very-?"

"Was you?" grinned Red. "I'll tell the cock-eyed world you was—stiff as a goat!"

A shamed flush spread over the girl's white face and mounted to the roots of her pale gold hair.

The uncomfortable pause that followed was finally broken by Red who said, "I'll get some coffee, that'll make yuh feel jake." She went out of the room, leaving the girl alone with her chaotic thoughts.

Betty Southerland sat up and looked about her. Who was this common, illiterate red-headed girl who had taken her in and shielded her from Tony, the handsome half-cast whom she had started out to flirt with simply to make Dick jealous. Dick, who was so uninterestingly proper. He was positively getting stodgy. She only wanted to philander a wee bit, but she had become fascinated beyond her own sane reasoning. She had taken too much to drink. She had not been herself. Ugh! What a rotten taste in her mouth. Her tongue felt furry. She ran it around the edge of her parched lips, and wondered vaguely what time it was. She must get home before Dick did. His ship was due tomorrow, no, today. He'd be furious if he knew about last night's escapade. He had made her promise not to go to Tijuana. There was already too much scandal about the young married women in their set whose indiscretions were getting their husbands into trouble with the Navy Department, and Dick was coming up for promotion to Commander, and she must be especially judicious at this time. Betty felt ashamed and very penitent and vowed she would never come again, she hadn't meant to in the first place for she really loved Dick, but he had been so peremptory in his order that she had rebelled—

Tijuana Red broke in on her retrospection, bearing a cup of steaming coffee which she handed to her. "Drink it, dearie, it'll keep the hangover from hangin' over too long."

"You're awfully good," murmured Betty gratefully, between sips.

Red shrugged depreciatively and turned to survey herself in the mirror. "Look like a hunk of cheese," she remarked with a rueful smile. "Well, soon as I get yuh out er this damn joint I'll pound the old ear 'till it gets dark." She yawned lustily.

Betty rose shakily and with Red's help managed to stagger into her clothes.

"Better put on some rouge, yuh look sorter bilious," suggested Red, handing her a small compact, and, as the girl hesitated, "it's all right, kid, I ain't used ut yet."

With a little embarrassed laugh Betty dusted some on her pale cheeks. "Thank you," she said, handing it back.

"Make ut snappy, dearie, I wanter get yuh outer here before anybody lamps yuh."

Red hustled her to a little battle-scarred bug that was drawn up alongside the curb with Danny sitting proudly at the wheel.

"Danny," admonished Red, "take good care of this poor Jane, an' don' stop fer nothin' 'til yuh land at San Diego, see?"

Betty put out her hand impulsively. "You haven't told me your name so I can write and thank you," she said graciously.

Red pretended not to see the friendly hand extended to her; she stuck hers into her pockets and stared at the ground as she answered a bit roughly, "aw, ferget ut—anyhow—I ain't got no name—exceptin'—Tijuana Red—they calls me."

RED CURLED HERSELF on the bed, her feet drawn up under her, the loose sleeves of her negligee falling away from the soft pink curves of her arms. She clasped her hands about her knees and gazed ardently at the tall man who was standing in front of the dresser with his gorgeously kimonoed back to her. He was parting and carefully brushing back his thick dark hair.

"Yeasus, sweet kid, this sure is the life, ain't ut, huh?" Joyously Red snapped her gum.

The man turned to her irritably. He was young, perhaps twenty-four or twenty-five and would have been handsome if his face hadn't borne the evident imprint of license. "I've told you before not to—chew—gum! It's a—rotten habit!"

"Yeasus, I fergot—but—I get the screamin' meemies sometimes an' just gotter do somethin'." She wet the end of her index finger and thumb and rolled the gum into a smooth ball between them and held it out to him. "Where'll I park ut, huh?"

"For God's sake, Red, don't stick it under any of the furniture!" he said with a grimace.

She looked at him reproachfully. "Yeasus, sweetie, I know better'n that." With which remark she sprang from the bed like a graceful feline and ran to the window.

He caught her upraised hand just in time. "My God, don't throw it out there!"

"Where the hell, then?" She glanced at him sidewise and gave his hand a little squeeze and began to giggle. "Oo—look at, look at, if the sweet kid ain't gone an' got stuck on me."

His eyes wavered from her fascinatingly piquant face to their hands stuck together with a mess of gum, and he scowled. "That's a damn vulgar trick," he said disgustedly and strode furiously to the bathroom.

Red took a prodigious breath and her eyes filled with sudden tears as she began to scrape off her share of the gum with her sharp pointed teeth, but her lips quickly quivered into a smile. "The kid don' mean nothin'. He's just nursin' a hangover," was her consoling thought. She cocked a loving ear toward the bathroom.

When he came out smiling a bit contritely she was lying on the bed, her hands clasped behind her head staring at the ceiling.

He went over to her and kissed her.

She drew him down beside her and ran her fingers through his hair. "Yeasus, sweet kid, ain't this the cat's purr?" she murmured contentedly.

He bent his head quickly and pressed his lips to the little warm hollow just beneath her chin on her white throat, to hide the frown that passed over his face.

She placed her two hands on his shoulders and held him away from her and stared intently and unsmilingly into his dark eyes. "Yeasus, kid, when I'm with yuh—I'm so happy—ut—hurts!"

A dark flush mounted in waves to his temples and suffused his eyes. He caught her in his arms and held her little palpitant body imprisoned there for a long moment. When at last he spoke his voice was husky with emotion. "You're a fascinating—baby," he said.

"Huh, I don't know 'bout bein' fascinatin' but I sure am some lovin' baby!" She wound her arms around his neck and pressed her warm moist lips hungrily to his. "Yuh know what I wisht, sweetie, huh?" And then he shook his head. "I wisht me an' yuh could have a swell little shack in San Diego—an' go on like this—forever. Wouldn't that be the cat's purr, huh?"

He drew away from her. "Don't be a fool, Red, you know we couldn't do that." His voice was coldly annoyed.

A hurt look came into her eyes and her lower lip began to quiver.

"For God's sake, don't cry. How I despise a sniveling woman!"

Tijuana Red swung her feet to the floor and sat up very straight. Two crimson spots burned on either cheekbone. "Don't get escared, Kid, I ain't goin' ter turn on the weeps. Nobody yet ever accused Tijuana Red of—ballin'. I was just remarkin'—how swell it ud be. I'm awful sick of playin' with a diffront bird every night—most of 'em drunker'n hell an' not knowin' what it's all about—just—animals—"

"You chose that kind of life, didn't you? It's nobody's fault but your own!" He glowered at her accusingly.

She smiled back at him as if he were a petulant child. "I ain't blamin' nobody. I liked ut before I met yuh—it was easier'n workin'."

"Well, what are you howling at then?"

"I ain't howlin', I just thought I'd like ter give ut up an' me an' yuh could—"

"Don't spring that marriage gag on me!"

She gazed at him with large reproving eyes and murmured in a low voice. "Aw, I know men like yuh don't marry girls—like—me. I don't expect nothin' like that. We don't have ter shimmie ter the tune of weddin' bells ter have a swell little shack—do we, huh?" She looked up at him eagerly but the little bubbling laugh that started in her heart ended in a harsh sort of gurgle in her throat and a sharp pained expression wiped out the sparkle in her eyes, leaving them dull and heavy.

The man turned from her irritably and strode to the window and looked into the street below. It was raining, not a hard cleansing rain to wash the filth from the earth, but a murky slow drizzle that mixed slimily with the oil from passing motors making it dangerously skiddy. With a shudder of revulsion he looked back at the girl. She was sitting very still on the edge of the bed, her hands clasped tightly about her knees. Her eyes, following his every move, had the expression of a faithful, worshipping canine in their red brown depths.

"Slime," he muttered.

Red started. "Meanin'—me!"

He shook his head, scowling. "Out there—it's slippery—unsafe!"

Red unclasped her hands and held them out to him. "Yeasus, sweet kid, yuh talk like you was coo-coo."

He ignored her outstretched hands and dug his own into his pockets. "This can't go on," he said laconically.

The girl paled and caught her lower lip between her teeth, and her voice shook a little when she asked. "Wadder yuh mean, this can't go on?"

"Exactly what I say. It's got to end—" And as she sprang up and came toward him. "For Heaven's sake, Red, don't make a scene!"

She stopped short. "Aw-I ain't goin' ter make no scene. Yuh just sort er—knocked me fer a loop." She walked unsteadily to the table and took a cigarette from a package that was lying there and with shaking fingers struck a match and lighted it. She took a few puffs, then smiled at him. "Yuh sure smacked the merry ha-ha plumb outer my system, kid—"

"I'm sorry, Red." His voice softened.

She came up to him and leaned her head against his arm. "Don't yuh want me no more—kid?"

"I only want you when I'm—drunk."

"An' that's mos' of the time."

He looked into her upturned face and his voice was harsh again when he spoke. "Red, you ought to understand. I never— loved you."

Her caressing hand dropped listlessly to her side and her half finished cigarette fell unheeded to the floor. Unconsciously the man put his heel on it. Red gazed at the black smudge it had left on the carpet before speaking. Finally she said with a bitter laugh tempered with humor. "I feel like that poor smoke. Yuh light me up an' I'm all aglow—then yuh step on me, an' I'm nothin' but a bunch of smutt—are yuh goin' first—or—do yuh want me ter?"

"I'll go—and here's a hundred, it's all I've got—"

"Aw—I don't want yuh money, kid."

"I'm sorry, Red—"

"Yuh needn't be—it ain't the first time Tijuana Red's been showed the gate—only—I—didn't love—none of those other birds."

"You'll get over it."

"Sure—s—say, I wisht yuh'd get ter hell out—before I bust out cryin'—"

When he had gone, Red reverted to type, first taking a huge slug of whisky which she had in a small flask in her sweater pocket, and, with her characteristic shrug she popped a whole package of gum into her mouth, five fresh sticks, one after the other, and chewing with much gusto, began to dress.

Dick Southerland paced the length of the living room and back before he stopped in front of his wife who sat huddled in one corner of the chesterfield, her hands clasped tightly in her lap, watching him with large frightened eyes.

He took the unlighted cigarette that he had been nervously chewing out of his mouth and spoke in his arrogant tone. "Betty, this is terrible! Suppose the Captain had found out?"

"B-but, he didn't," protested Betty weakly.

"He might have, and if he had it would cost me my commission!"

"W-why worry about something that hasn't happened? I—I'm awfully sorry, Dick."

"Being sorry won't stop those old tabbies from talking! You gave me your word, why did you break it?"

Betty dropped her eyes before his accusing ones and a shamed flush suffused her face.

Her husband's lip curled in a half sneer. "The whole affair was disgraceful! Don't you know it's against regulations for officers to go to Tijuana?"

"I'm—I'm not an—officer."

"You're an officer's wife, it's the same thing. Whatever you do reflects on me!"

Betty sat silent clasping and unclasping her long tapering fingers.

Dick lighted his cigarette and began pacing the floor again. Suddenly he stopped. "Where did you spend the night?" he shot at her unexpectedly.

Betty jumped. "Why—I—I—the border was closed and I—had to stay—there—"

"Where's—there?"

"Why—Tijuana—of course."

"Alone?"

"Yes—no—"

"What do you mean, 'yes—no'?"

"Why—a—a—girl took care of me—I was very ill—"

"Are you quite sure it was a—girl?"

Betty raised her head proudly. "Be careful, Dick Southerland!" she warned.

A moment of silence, then, "what girl—one of the party?"

"N—no—just a girl—down there."

"How did it happen that just a girl happened to stay there?"

"She didn't 'happen to stay,' she lives there."

"Lives there? There are no *decent* girls who live there!"

"Maybe not—but this one was decent—to me."

"Huh—that's very likely—what was her name?"

"I don't know, but they call her, Tijuana Red."

"My God!"

Betty sat up very straight and asked with polite virulence, "do you know her?"

He moistened his dry lips. "Know her? Of course not! Except by reputation, she's notorious, and you stayed all night with that woman! Why she isn't fit to touch the shoe of a respectable girl! My God, Betty, she's bad!"

"Her morals may be bad but her heart is good. She kept me—from harm!"

"Kept you from harm? What do you mean? You had better go to your mother until this blows over. A divorce and scandal at this time might hinder my promotion."

Betty sprang to her feet, paling. "A divorce?" she cried, staring at him incredulously, "what do you mean?"

There was a moment of tense silence, the one waiting for the other, finally Dick said with a grimace of contempt, "how do I know you're telling the truth?"

The color flamed in her cheeks and the pupils of her cornflower blue eyes suddenly widened, making them appear almost black. "How dare you insinuate that I—oh!" She put her fingers quickly to her lips to hide their trembling.

Dick took an involuntary step backward and put out his hand as if to ward off the onslaught of her unleased anger. "My dear, you misunderstood me. I was only thinking of my promotion—"

"Your promotion, your promotion!" she screamed, "that's all you ever do think of! Yourself and your promotion! You think more of that than you do of your—wife!" She rushed from the room in a deluge of hurt, outraged tears.

Dick Southerland stood scowling, irresolute, the cigarette smoking, unheeded between his fingers. This was worse than he had expected. What a damn fool he had been! Betty was sensitive and high-spirited. He was afraid to think what she might do now. He should have been more gentle, more tactful. He bungled where he should have used diplomacy—and—he really loved Betty in his selfish, arrogant way. God, what a fool he'd been! He took his handkerchief out of his pocket and wiped away the beads of cold perspiration that started out on his brow. His head was spinning, his thoughts whirling around in a mad circle.

The gray ash from his cigarette dropped to the floor and the hot glowing cinders burned themselves out against his hand. He started with the sharp sting of it and let it drop, and with a strange smile twisting his lips, watched the blisters slowly forming between his fingers.

"YOU'RE A GOOD kid, Danny—too good fer me." Tijuana Red smiled affectionately at Danny between thoughtful smacks of her wad of chewing gum.

Danny's genial round countenance was puckered into a ludicrous frown in an effort to look as serious as his thoughts were. He held tightly to one of her hands and his words tumbled over each other in his endeavor to get them out before he lost courage. "They ain't no man livin', Red, too good fer yuh, an' I mean straight by yuh, kid, wid a parson an' all the trimmin's, an' a slick little shack in San Diego. I got a good pile too an' a swell honest bootleggin' job waitin' fer me, wid big Murph as pardner. All yuh got ter do, kid, is say the woird." It was a long speech for Danny and his highly colored face turned a shade more rufos with the unusual exertion, and with the back of his hand he wiped away the perspiration that dripped from his forehead.

"Yeasus, Danny, yuh sure drooled a bib-full, an' I'm that

blowed up, but honest, kid, I wouldn't spoil yuh life fer yuh—an'—an'—yus nice *honest* job of bootleggin'." Red's mouth twitched and the tiny lines around her russet eyes crinkled in a humorous smile, but for the first time there was no spontaneity in Danny's sober mien as he answered,

"Yuh couldn't spoil my life, Red, yuh'd make ut fer me! God, if it wasn't fer yuh I'der quit long ago, I ain't fergot how yuh grub-staked me when I first come down—a common, sneakin' bum, half starved an' sick an' bitter, fresh from servin' ten years in the pen—"

"Aw, ferget ut, Danny, that wasn't nothin'," she interrupted, drawing her hand away. "Look at the swell job yuh got now, ain't yuh satisfied?"

"Sure, if yuh'd trot in double harness wid me." His hopeful expression suddenly clouded. "S-say, kid, yuh ain't soft on the brass-button bird?"

Tijuana Red was silent and even stopped her nervous munching of her gum as she gazed dreamily into the bar mirror in her characteristic pose, one foot on the brass rail, right hand on her hip, left elbow resting on the bar and her hand supporting her head.

Danny watched her intently.

At last she shook her head slowly and a rueful smile lightly touched her lips. "It wouldn' do me no good, Danny, he give me the air."

Danny doubled up his fists and looked as fierce as his benign moon face would permit. "I'll knock his damn block off fer 'im!" He threatened.

"Naw, Danny, it wouldn' do no good. Tijuana Red savies when she's beat." With a sudden movement she rested both hands on the bar, palms down. "Say, kid, what's the odds on your little filly?"

Danny's face broke into an enthusiastic grin. "Fifteen ter one shot, an' Red, I'll tell the cock-eyed world, she's a wow, fast as a crow an' only 101 pounds in the saddle."

"Whose ridin' 'er?"

"Little Mickey Higgins, an' s-say that kid ain't bigger'n a grass-hopper's ear."

"Yeh, I know 'im. Some jock! You're lucky ter get 'im. Say, how'll I play 'er?"

"Play 'er ter win."

Red looked at him dubiously. "Yuh ain't razzin' me, Danny?"

"I'm handin' ut ter yuh straight, kid, s'help me—"

"Maybe it ud be safer ter play 'er ter show, huh?" Red snapped her gum in deep thought.

"Play 'er ter win!" insisted Danny.

For a space Red seemed to ponder, then, "All right, Danny," and stooping, she took a roll of grimy green-backs out of the top of her rolled stocking just above the garnet silk and black lace garter, and threw them on the bar. "Count 'em, Danny, three hundred berries. I been savin' fer this race, an' I'll lay muh las' copper on that cute little two year ole of your's. Danny, what's the lady's name?"

Danny leaned across the bar and whispered in Red's ear.

"Yeasus!" ejaculated Red. "Now, ain't that the cat's purr? Set 'em up, kid, the drink's is on me."

Danny pocketed the roll of bills and filled two glasses with whiskey, shoving one toward Red and holding the other in his hand.

The girl took the gum out of her mouth and held it dexterously between her thumb and pointing finger, while with the other hand she reached for the glass. "Here's ter Tijuana Red," she cried gayly and with one gulp swallowed her whiskey straight.

"Ter both of 'em, they's winners," echoed Danny with a pleased smirk.

There was a moment of silence in which each eyed the other reflectively. Then Danny spoke again. "Yuh'll think about what I was sayin', kid?" With a quirk of his lips he managed a pathetic smile.

Red nodded, and suddenly popped the gum back into her mouth. "If your little filly wins, Danny, me boy, I'm yours fer life. Are yuh game?"

"I'll tell the cock-eyed world!"

Red stuck her hands in her pockets and swaggered to the swinging doors. "S'long," she laughed over her shoulder and was gone.

THE HORSES WERE in the paddock nervously straining at their handlers who were walking them in circles preparatory to the opening race at Tijuana.

The bookies scribbled busily on their pads. It promised to be a big day. The betting was heavy. Not a cloud marred the warm blueness of the sky and the sun smiled brightly on the colorful assemblage that crowded the bleachers, the club-house veranda and lawn. The turf was hard and fast.

Tijuana Red and Danny elbowed their way through the seething good natured mass of humanity to the fence that enclosed the race track. Here they stopped and leaned on it, one foot on the lowest rail, much as they would a bar. Danny took out his field glasses and Red chewed vigorously on her inevitable wad of gum.

The post bugle sounded; the air was charged with suppressed excitement as the horses took their places.

"They're off!"

The gallery watched with that breath arresting tenseness of a calm before the storm, starting with a confused mumble, increasing in volume and finally crashing into a mighty roar.

Danny's little bay filly got a bad start, it being her first race, but she soon got her stride and caught Miss Judy before the half was reached and dashing to the front, won without being extended. She had three lengths to spare over You-tell-em, the favorite, at the final wire.

Red, forgetting for the moment to chew, her hands doubled up in tight fists in her sweater pockets, leaned far over the top rail of the fence.

The gallery broke into a mad jumble of sound.

"Yeasus!" exclaimed Tijuana Red, looking at Danny uncertainly.

He was mopping his face and neck with a huge, gorgeously colored silk kerchief, and a Cheshire-Cat like grin sat drolly upon his plump red countenance. He caught her arm. "You're mine fer keeps, kid," he whispered a bit hoarsely.

Red's mouth sagged open but she contrived a feeble smile. "I hope ter shout!" she said, managing a small semblance of enthusiasm.

Danny squeezed her hand. "I'll buy yuh anything yuh want fer a engagement present, just name ut, an' ut's your's."

"Aw, Danny, ain't yuh the sweet daddy, though? C'on let's get soused." Red's laugh rose shrilly above the babble.

"Sure, me an' yuh both," chuckled Danny.

Arm in arm they sauntered toward the Casino, Red with her familiar swagger and Danny with his little short mincing steps, almost running to keep up with her.

Just over the threshold of the Casino Tijuana Red halted abruptly, and with a well aimed, long distance spat her wad of chewing gum landed with a soft plop in the nearest cuspidor.

Danny, sensing that something was wrong, eyed her intently and unconsciously closed his fingers more tightly over her arm.

For one fleeting instant a cloud passed over the natural brilliance of Red's russet irids, as they rested on a man sitting alone at a small inconspicuous table in one corner of the Casino. A dissonant laugh forced its way through her dry lips as she moved forward. "C'on, Danny, we gotter celebrate," she cried in her high pitched, carrying voice.

The man at the table in the corner looked up and his gaze held hers, but he did not smile. He gave an imperceptible shrug and turned away with no sign of recognition.

At the bar Tony was suavely blending potent tequila with the insidious langour of his smoldering black eyes as he lounged across the mahogany bar, very close to the pale gold beauty of Betty Southerland whose delicate flower-like cheeks were tinged with a hectic flush, and whose flutelike laughter was garbled with intoxication.

Danny and Red reached the bar in time to hear Tony's low whisper, "My beautiful golden señora, you will meet me in the patio of the Little Adobe when the clock chimes the hour of midnight?" And as Betty Southerland seemed to hesitate he added quickly. "I will give to you the handsome rebozo that belonged to my grandmother."

Danny edged closer to Red and whispered, "If Rose catches 'em she'll stick her stilleto in his black heart."

"Or, maybe her's," Red murmured inaudibly. "Set 'em up, Tony," she called aloud, "Danny's buyin' fer the crowd."

The Mexican half-cast straightened with a jerk and eyed Red venomously but she stared him down. He shifted his gaze uneasily and began nervously to set the glasses on the bar.

Betty Southerland looked from Tony to Tijuana Red and smiled uncertainly. " 'Lo," she said tipsily, swaying toward Red.

"How's tricks?" returned Red, saluting. "Any luck at the races?"

Betty wagged her head and began fumbling in the depths of her beaded bag that was hanging on her arm. At last she extracted a huge roll of bills and held it up proudly. "Played Tijuana Red 'cause it's your name an' won five hundred!" Her voice was growing a little thick.

With a quick impulsive motion Red seized the bills and thrust them back into Betty's bag. "Yeasus, dearie, don' flash that wad er Jewish flags 'round here! Somebody'll snitch 'em offen yuh." She sent Tony a significant look and picked up her glass. "Here's mud in yuh eye," she laughed swallowing her whiskey.

Danny followed suit, and after a stare of dumb amazement at Red, Betty giggled inanely and reached for her glass.

A crowd gathered about the bar and Danny bought another round of drinks.

"Gotter beat ut back ter woirk," he announced when he had drained his glass. "Comin', kid?" This last was addressed to Red, who shook her head.

"Hell, no, the fight's just startin'."

Danny was crestfallen and she temporized with, "Later—maybe."

After Danny had gone, Tijuana Red left the bar and wandered disinterestedly around the gaming tables and finally gravitated toward the small table in its secluded corner with its lone occupant.

The man looked up as she approached him. He seemed older and his face was haggard, his eyes heavy-lidded that bespoke of many sleepless nights, rather than dissipation.

Red's heart contracted and her throat ached as she regarded him, but she smiled and gave her careless salute as she eased into the chair opposite him. "How's tricks?" was her greeting.

He stared at her unsmilingly.

Red wriggled uncomfortably. "My, but ain't he the chummy bird?" she inquired of the air, then she leaned suddenly across the table and stared intently into his face. "Hell, yuh ain't the bird I thought yuh was!" Her baffled expression drew a wan smile from the man.

"No." He answered her mute question. "I'm Ray's older brother, Dick."

"Yeasus!" Red slumped back in her chair, the animation dying out of her face.

The man sat silently, his elbows resting on the table, his hands supporting his head as if it were too heavy to hold itself erect.

Red lighted a cigarette, took a few puffs and tamped it out. "Ray's parson brother," she murmured.

The man said nothing.

She leaned toward him. "What's eatin' yuh?" She demanded unexpectedly.

The man moistened his dry lips. "You're a—good—kid—

Red. Ray—told—me—about—you." He spoke with an effort, as if against his will and his eyes shifted from her compassionate face to the bar at the farther end of the Casino and back again. "Perhaps—you—can help me."

Red's laugh rose on a surprised sharp note. "Me—help—you? Yeasus!"

The man leaned toward her. "I'm in trouble, Red, will you help me?" His tone was so low that Red had to watch his lips to understand what he was saying.

She nodded. "Yuh know me, bo. I ain't never refused ter help a—buddy yet."

"I wonder if you can?" He mused half aloud, studying her intently.

"Sure I can. Go ahead. Shoot!"

A long silence fell between them. The man's attention was held by someone at the bar and he seemed to have forgotten entirely the existence of the girl who sat watching him in the chair opposite. Her eyes never left his face. Her hand fumbled nervously in her sweater pocket and her fingers closed over a new package of gum, but they loosened and came out empty. She tapped her foot, keeping time to the music, and finally motioned to a waiter. "One tequila and a whiskey straight," she ordered.

The man's eyes came back to her with a jerk and he smiled rather forlornly. "I've made an awful ass of myself," he confessed.

Red lighted a cigarette and took a few puffs before answering. "Sure—most men do." She nodded sagely.

His attention turned again to the bar. Red's eyes followed his.

"See—that—pretty—blond—girl, drinking and—flirting with that damn spig bar-tender?" His voice was strained with his endeavor to keep it from trembling.

"Yuh sweetie, I getcher."

"My—wife!"

Red's cigarette fell from nerveless fingers and her mouth sagged open. "Yeasus," she breathed.

"I—drove her from me with my arrogance, my smug preaching. I drove—her—to that. God!" He shook impotent fists at the ceiling, then his arms dropped heavily to the table and his head sank upon them while his whole frame shook with silent sobs.

Red gazed at him dumbly, her mind able to comprehend his suffering, but her tongue powerless to utter her thoughts or to even formulate any words of sympathy and understanding, and so she sat watching and waiting for—she knew not what, her heart sick within her.

At last he lifted his head. "Perhaps it isn't too late to save her from—him—from—herself. Will you help me?"

Red swallowed the lump in her throat that threatened to strangle her. "Will a tiger fight fer her cub?" She finally managed to articulate, and lower and rather wonderingly, "Ray's parson brother."

A look of relief crossed his harassed features and he smiled wanly at her.

She pushed the glass of tequila over to him. "Gargle that, kid, it'll put hair on yuh chest." She swallowed her liquor, wiping her mouth on the back of her hand, and rose. "Got the time on yuh?"

He glanced at his watch. "Seven-thirty," he answered, watching her curiously and half rising from his chair.

She motioned him back. "Savie the Little Adobe?" she asked him.

Ray had taken him there on the first and only time he had ever crossed the border.

He nodded assent.

"Meet me there, in the patio, at midnight."

"Why—there?" he asked in surprise.

"Don' ast me no questions."

"Red," he admonished, "this is no time to arrange for a lover's trysting place."

She looked at him blankly. "A lovers' wot kind of a place? I don' know what it's all about, but I'll tell the cock-eyed world I ain't nobody's dumb Dora!"

Dick Southerland hitched his chair irritably. "We're wasting time," he snapped impatiently.

"*Yuh* might be but *I* ain't, s'long." She started off.

"Wait!" He commanded.

She came back to him and leaned over his shoulder. "Don' yuh trust me, kid?" she whispered, a catch in her voice.

"Y-yes," he answered a bit reluctantly.

"I savie wot I'm doin' an' remember this, kid, Tijuana Red ain't never yet double-crossed a Buddy!" Without another word she pushed her hands into her pockets and swaggered across the Casino and through the doors into the mystical night beyond.

The Little Adobe, with its flower-laden patio, hidden behind a high Spanish wall, stood on a narrow crooked back street of Old Town. Pedro, its owner, abided there alone. "Blind Pedro," they called him, on account of his poor sightless eyes. He was old and withered and bent. Even those Mexicans, halfbreeds and derelicts who lived in Old Town rarely visited Pedro, and the Americanos were a bit wary of wandering away from the one main street of the wicked little settlement to seek adventure in its dark portentous byways. Tony had chosen the rendezvous for its seclusion. He had taken Betty Souther-land there in the afternoon before the races and she had been enchanted with its quaintness and the beauty of its old fash-ioned garden.

Tijuana Red glided swiftly and silently along the lonely winding streets, darting in and out among the shadows like a phantom, now and then pausing to listen to make sure that she was not being followed.

At the little gate, mellowed to a soft green by the hot rays of the sun and many rains that swung into the patio on tough rawhide hinges, she lingered a moment, every nerve taut. She could hear Pedro moving about inside the house and see the flicker of his candle as he shuffled from the long low room that served as his living and dining-room to his sleeping quarters adjoining. Soon the candle was snuffed out and quiet reigned within.

Softly Red pushed open the gate and stole into the patio. There was no moon and the flowers, the miniature lily-pond in the center, the ancient sun-dial and stone benches shrank into the shadows like ghosts. To the blackest corner where a large clump of cactus spread its hardy prickly fin-like leaves, she moved without sound and watched with eyes that pene-trated the gloom like a cat's. Hardly daring to breathe she leaned against the adobe wall and awaited the coming of Betty Southerland and Tony.

A half hour passed, perhaps an hour, Red had no way of telling, when the little green gate swung noiselessly in and the uncertain steps of a girl sounded lightly on the stone walk.

Red came out from her hiding place and was beside Betty before she realized that she was not alone.

"Don' scream," cautioned Red.

Which was just what Betty intended doing, but she gulped instead. "Wha-what are you doing here?"

"If I wasn' a perfec' lady I'd ast yuh the same thing, but I ain't no snob so I'll tell yuh. I come ter meet my sweetie."

"Oh," rather blankly from Betty.

"Listen, kid," went on Red, drawing Betty with her behind the sheltering cactus. "Tony ain't goin' ter meet yuh here fer no good reason."

Betty drew herself up with frigid dignity. "I don't understand what you are referring to," she said stiffly.

"Aw—sure—yuh do—an' I ain't got no time ter argue. Yuh hubby'll be here any minute an' I'll tell the cock-eyed world he's been eatin' raw meat. He's wild!"

"I don't believe you!" Betty's indignant voice rose shrilly.

"Sh—" warned Red.

Betty's eyes turned swiftly to the little green gate.

"Quick, give me yuh cape an' hat," whispered Red, taking off her own sweater and rakish tam and thrusting them into Betty's trembling hands.

The gate opened cautiously and the dark figure of a man prowled into the garden.

"Señora?" came in Tony's caressing purr.

Red gave Betty's arm a warning pinch and glided toward the half-cast.

"Yes," she said softly.

"Ah, señora." Tony peered through the gloom at the wraith-like figure before him. "Your coming is proof that you love me, is it not so, my golden señora?"

"Yes," murmured Red moving nearer.

He held out his arms and drew the unresisting girl to his palpitating heart. It was an easier conquest than he had anticipated. Women were all alike, no matter of what people. He chuckled with pleasurable anticipation. He hoped she still had the five hundred pesos with her that she had won at the races. He surely had gained a golden prize!

The girl wound her arms tightly about his neck and pressed closer to him.

Dios Mio, she had the passion of his own hot-blooded ancestors!

He bent his head and kissed her upon her mouth.

Suddenly from out of the darkness sprang Rose. Her right arm was upraised and something long and sharp gleamed in her hand, as with a snarl of rage of some untamed beast, she lunged forward. Quick as she was Red was quicker as with a swift motion Red's right foot shot out behind her catching Rose in the knee and driving her back with unexpected suddenness.

"Dios Mio!" cried Tony, his eyes shifting in fascinated horror from Red who had wriggled out of his arms and sunk silently to the ground, to that of the distorted features of Rose.

She laughed crazily and tossed the stiletto into the bushes. "Mucho bueno, 'golden señora,' bah!" She spat on Red's motionless figure and disappeared in the gloom. The darkness swallowing her as if by some strange magic.

Then Betty's terrified scream rent the ominous silence that followed. She screamed again and again until the stifled atmosphere vibrated with her cries.

Pedro, his hands stretched out before him and his blind eyes staring into the darkness, groped his way into the garden. "Dios Mio, what has happened?" he cried in his feeble voice.

The confused scuffle of running feet sounded from the street outside and a muttering of excited voices in a strange mixture of many tongues. The little green gate was pushed violently open and Dick Southerland, closely followed by Danny, rushed into the patio.

Betty precipitated herself into her husband's arms sobbing hysterically. He held her tightly, smoothing her hair. "What is it? What is it?" he murmured trying to calm her.

Danny knelt beside the motionless figure and gently turned it over and his pocket flashlight outlined Red's still face, pale as death in the ghostly circle and a great sob tore at his throat.

"Red, dear little kid," he cried brokenly, "speak to me. Yuh—yuh ain't—dead?"

"Hell, no!" She sat up suddenly, an impish grin twitching her lips, "but, yeasus, Danny, I was damn scared!"

She scrambled to her feet and took Danny's arm.

"Danny, me boy," she said a bit shakily. "That slick little shack in San Diego with the swell honest bootleggin' job listens like the cat's pur to Tijuana Red!"

Hell-Bent for Tia Juana

Wishbone was small of stature, or he could hardly have been a jockey. But he also stuttered which made him sensitive and retiring, and inclined people to take advantage of him, little guessing the heart behind his gentle manner and the dynamite he packed in each fist.

HE WAS LITTLE, about five feet five, and his spindly legs were bowed. His hair was blond and sleek like pulled taffy. His eyes, cornflower blue, round and expressionless, resembling a china doll's. His features—small, almost effeminate. His skin velvety with a soft rose glow spreading from the rather high cheekbones to the edge of his jaw, and only in the bright sunlight could a faint honey-colored down be distinguished upon his upper lip and around his pointed chin.

"Wishbone," they called him, probably because he was shaped like one, but above the narrow waist-line rippled a network of powerful, steel-like muscles hardly to be suspected in one of so slight build. If he had ever had any other name it had been lost somewhere in transit.

He had only recently come to Tia Juana, imported from the vast and shadowy regions of the cattle country to jockey for the mysterious owner of Hell-Bent, the big chestnut gelding—a raw-boned four-year-old with the head and disposition of a mule.

The evening before the opening of the races in the border town, Wishbone jogged despondently along the rough dirt road. His thoughts troubled him, for he had left home without telling Nanny where he was going. He was taking a long chance, but he was desperate. Money he must have! Heaps of it! He crossed the rickety wooden bridge that hung dejectedly over the parched river-bed, and into the sordid atmosphere of Old Town. A filthy little settlement with one short main street

that boasted a newly paved road, either side of which huddled a series of one-story saloons and dance-halls, a wanton challenge to the senses—openly defiant.

The dark curtain of night had already been drawn across the face of the sun, and the wicked saturnine lights flashed their insensate message to those mad seekers of pleasure who fled to the border to sink their souls in the black well of human weakness.

He had worked Hell-Bent on the track that afternoon and the big horse had developed a startling new trick of taking the bit and running when Wishbone wanted to hold him under restraint, and of slowing when he gave him the signal to speed up. This strange contrariness worried Wishbone. Now he wanted to return to his room at the Turf Bar and rest and try to figure out some tactics by which he could control this headstrong racer.

He passed the San Francisco Cantina, the Tivoli Bar, Gonzales Cantina, Alhambra Café, the Gringo hot-dog stand—where he answered the friendly flourish of a pancake-turner in the hand of the big American with his guileless smile—passed the fly-specked, dust-besmeared Mexican curio store, the Log Cabin, and went on to the Turf Bar, the last ramshackle dump to withstand the onslaught of rum-thirsty pirates.

Before the half-swinging doors that led into the ribald room beyond, Wishbone hesitated. His hands were in his trousers pockets as he slowly swung the doors open with an elbow and shoulder movement. Into the liquor-soaked air of the room stepped the little jockey. The long mahogany bar was polished like the face of a mirror by the rubbing of many elbows, the accompanying brass rail polished by the soles of many feet. The opposite side was lined with slot machines; beyond, another pair of swinging doors led into a dance-hall, the hardwood floor in the center surrounded by tables, in one corner a small platform where a negro band blared forth its heathenish ideas of Jasmania. Wishbone paused, a look of mild surprise suffusing his innocent countenance. To one who knew him, it was an expression quite characteristic, that might mean everything—or nothing, but to a stranger it registered only one thing—physical cowardice.

And there was a stranger lolling against the bar tonight. A big, beefy hulk of a man with heavy features and small, shifty, colorless eyes. He gulped his whiskey neat with a tumbler of beer for a chaser, and regarded Wishbone with the sneering grin of the bully for an under-dog. "Ho-ho there, cutie," he bellowed. "Come here and have one on me."

Wishbone shook his head, still smiling blandly, his hands in his pockets.

"Aw come on, cutie; don't be bashful," the stranger urged, his voice rising, blustering.

The men and the girls at the bar stopped talking, their glasses held in tensing fingers, watching—waiting. And those at the slot machines paused in the act of twirling the wheel and watched curiously. There was something vaguely threatening underlying the stranger's rough camaraderie.

Wishbone stared at him in round-eyed wonder.

"Ah—ah—I don't drink," he replied, in his peculiarly hesitating speech, his artless smile belying the bluntness of his refusal.

The giant threw back his head and roared, his raucous laugh echoing and re-echoing through the tensely silent room. He pounded his huge hairy fist on the bar until the glasses rattled and trembled like terror-stricken children.

"'Ah—-ah—I don't drink,'" he mimicked. "Maybe you'd like a cup of hot milk, dearie?" he simpered, then added suddenly, vehemently, "Hell! Step up to the bar like a reg'lar he-man and swill some hooch. It might put hair on that sunken-in chest er yours!" He glanced around at the watchers, hushed, motionless—his thick lips twisted in a nasty grin.

Wishbone stood immobile, his bowed legs spread apart, his hands in his pockets, his expression slightly bewildered. "Th-thanks, stranger, b-but I never drink," he repeated softly.

The big man turned to the bartender, a puffy, greasy Mexican.

"Can you feature that, Salvy-door? The cute little thing refuses to drink. Well, well, we'll see. Set 'em up, Salvy-door." Swiftly, for so heavy a man, the stranger wheeled and in two long strides was by the little jockey's side. His small, shifty eyes glowered down into the round, expressionless orbs raised, with that slightly surprised stare, to his.

Wishbone stood perfectly still beneath the giant towering over him.

A few frightened gasps from some of the girls, a moment of breath-arresting tensity—then with a swooping motion the stranger grasped Wishbone by the seat of his trousers and the collar of his coat and rushed him to the bar. "Now, lap up your dish of cream, you miserable little puppy, or by God, I'll smash you to a pulp!" He held him up so that his feet dangled helplessly an inch above the brass rail. The tenseness of the atmosphere broke, the onlookers laughed, they giggled, they roared. The stranger glanced at his audience and guffawed with them.

Then Wishbone made a sudden, unexpected squirm, twisted free of the stranger's grasp, his hands fisting as they jerked out of his pockets. His left arm swept swiftly forward with a short, hard jab that landed with the force of a locomotive on the point of the big man's chin and he went down like a felled ox—inert, senseless.

"I said—ah—ah—I didn't drink," murmured the little jockey, pocketing his hands and pushing his way through the swinging doors with his characteristic elbow and shoulder movement.

Fifteen counts later the stranger came to—groggily—bleerily. "What the hell hit me?" he demanded weakly, fingering gingerly of his swollen jaw.

"I t'ink I hear some place dat dee leetle jock you was razzin' is a—ex-pug," calmly stated Salvador.

"Hell!" remarked the stranger, feelingly.

WISHBONE RAN HIS trained, sensitive fingers along the big chestnut's forelegs with a gentle, lingering touch. The gelding nosed him with his soft muzzle and winced slightly as the jockey's prying hand found a small swelling just beneath the left shoulder.

"Huh, you've went an' got one er them shoe-boils again." Wishbone spoke softly as he massaged the animal's legs. "We jest gotter win these here two races, Hell-Bent, thet we're booked fer. One of 'em anyhow. Nanny'll be powerful disappointed if she don't git ter go ter thet there man in Germany, an' wot other chanct has a runty bow-legged jock got ter git thet much jack?"

Rivers, the new trainer, hovered in the background, watching Wishbone with narrowed, cunning eyes.

"Hell-Bent ain't feelin' so good today," he remarked, coming over and standing beside the little jockey. "Too bad you gotter race him."

Wishbone straightened and smiled his guileless smile. "Ah— ah—he's all right. We'll win easy, won't we, old timer?" He stroked the chestnut's glistening neck.

"Why don't you get him scratched? He's the most ornery cuss I ever seen when he ain't feelin' good."

"N-never say die's my motto," answered Wishbone blithely, hopping into the saddle, but he went to the post with an unaccustomed feeling of foreboding.

It was raining, a sort of half-hearted drizzle. The air was heavy, depressing. The turf, wet and soggy.

The grandstand and club lawn were crowded with racegoers, their gay-colored sports clothes looking a bit tawdry in the cloudy light and shrieking in blatant defiance at the somberness of the day.

The fence enclosing the track was jammed with the usual race-horse touts, hangers-on, driftage from the undercurrents of the world, with their painted faces, hollow, lusterless eyes, and set, railing carmined lips. A mass of humans unrelated, yet interfused for the moment with a single purpose.

"They're off!" The cry struck the stillness like an overwhelming breaker bursting with all its fury against a rocky shore, then suddenly ceased as if some huge hand had stifled it.

Hell-Bent refused to break when the carrier was sprung and was left flat-footed at the post, the rest of the field scampering away in front. Wishbone humped over the big chestnut's neck, courageously urging the animal forward, finally picking up and passing the leaders one after the other until he reached the saddle-skirts of Big Ben, the favorite.

Then suddenly Hell-Bent swerved cut, taking the middle of the track. Wishbone used all his force to pull him to the rail, but the powerful horse refused to be guided. A trailing horse caught up with him, splashing mud in their faces as he raced past. Wishbone set his lips grimly, struggling with all his skill and knowledge to combat the stubborn will of Hell-Bent. He never carried a whip and wouldn't have used it if he had. The gelding began to lag, losing all interest in the race. Three horses galloped to the finish line ahead of him.

Wishbone dropped his head down on the gelding's lathered neck and great silent sobs shook his small body. "Why did yuh double-cross me, old timer?" he mumbled, his quivering lips pressed close to Hell-Bent. "I know yuh got the heart. I don't git it. I jest don't git it!"

Hell-Bent's head drooped and his ears lopped down like a dejected mule's.

The groom, a freckled-faced lad of fifteen with a wide mouth and humorous light blue eyes, came up, caught the horse by the bridle and led him toward the stables. "Gee-gosh, Wishbone, it's a darn crime! What ails the hoss—he acts all in?"

The little jockey raised his head and his lips trembled into a pathetic, child-like smile.

"Ah—it's all in the game, Alex," he answered noncommittally. He slid to the floor and ran his hands along the thoroughbred's legs. They bent in weakly at the knees. He was breathing hard and his sturdily muscled flanks were quivering. He seemed exhausted—spent.

Wishbone snatched the blanket from Rivers who had sauntered up almost reluctantly, as if he were in no hurry to cover the shivering animal.

"Told you to scratch that horse. He ain't fit to race," he said glumly.

Alex gave the man a quick, keen glance as he led Hell-Bent to his stall.

Wishbone paid no heed, he was busy with his own chaotic thoughts; there was a puzzled frown between his mild blue eyes as he hurried to the jockey-room.

He began changing his colored silks and highly polished boots for his nondescript tan riding breeches, gray sweater and tan puttees, unconscious of the riders around him. He didn't speak to them. He never had entered into their good-natured conversation. He didn't make friends easily. There was no aloofness in his manner, but rather a pathetic aloneness. He would smile at them vaguely, giving them the impression of a child who wants to play with the other boys but doesn't dare.

A shadow fell across the room and Navarro, squat of figure and swarthy of skin, made his ill-omened appearance. His black hair clustered in oily ringlets over his bullet-shaped head, his eyes were black and round and cruel like a snake's. Navarro, the Mexican superintendent of the track, with his huge chest puffed out like an inflated balloon.

The good-humored banter of the riders ceased abruptly as his hulk darkened the doorway. He stood just across the threshold, his pudgy thumbs stuck into the armholes of his black and white checked vest, his shoe-button eyes searching out Wishbone who stood at the farther end of the room. They caught and held the calm blue orbs of the little jockey.

"Say, you!" he shouted. "What the hell you mean by pullin' that race!"

The riders glanced in startled apprehension from the Mexican to Wishbone, standing within their midst and yet apart, erect, his spindly bowed legs spread wide, his hands in his trouser pockets, his face serene.

"Ah—ah—yuh ain't by any chanct addressin' yuh remarks ter—me?" he inquired in mild surprise.

"The hell I ain't! Yuh pulled that race! I seen you, an' anyways I got other proof!"

"I—ah—ah—sure don't know wot got inter Hell-Bent. He acts—kinder—low," Wishbone argued patiently, ignoring the insult of the superintendent.

Navarro glared, his beady eyes snapping menacingly.

The riders stood motionless, waiting tensely for the little jockey's death-knell.

"You don' know! Well I know! You sneakin' leetle liar! You pulled that race, an' I'll have you warned off, see!" How he managed to get there so quickly, no one seemed to remember, but Wishbone was suddenly standing close to Navarro, looking him unflinchingly in the eye, a stare of child-like wonder spreading over his face, a slight smile hovering about his lips.

"Y—yes—I see," he answered softly. One! Two! His fists

shot out unexpectedly like piston-rods, a quick left jab, a right cross, landing with startling rapidity on the hidden point of the Mexican's round, squashy chin. He went out more quietly than he had come in. Wishbone hurdled the inert form, lying like a lump of soft mud on the floor, and turned to the riders grouped together, in the middle of the room, with gaping mouths.

"I—ah—ah—sure hated ter do it, but I—ah—don't allow nobody ter call me a—liar," he explained softly, with an apologetic grin.

IN THE HUSH of the gray morning that followed, Wishbone crouched in the hay, his blond head pillowed in his out-flung arms against the friendly warmth of the gelding's side.

Alex usually slept in the stall with the horse, but Wishbone had taken his place the night before, saying, "Yuh hop over ter my diggin's an' sleep on a cotton mattress fer a change." His smile had been so pathetically pleading that Alex had consented, for he understood the little jockey better than anyone, unless, perhaps, it was Hell-Bent himself. Unknown to Wishbone, Alex many a time had heard him talking to the big chestnut, not as if he were a four-legged dumb beast, but a man with the intelligence to understand and the heart to sympathize.

Alex had come from the same little cattle town in Idaho where Wishbone had learned to ride and had worshipped the agile little cowpuncher from the vast difference of ten years. In those earlier days, it thrilled his child's heart to be the one chosen above all the cowboys to be talked to almost as if he were a grown man himself. Later and quite by accident he discovered the reason for Wishbone's preference. Wishbone had two great handicaps to overcome. One was his small stature with his rather aesthetic features, which he counteracted by becoming the featherweight champion of his state. But the other he never could quite conquer; he was painfully conscious of the fact that he stuttered.

In his sensitiveness he avoided the other cowboys and spent his time with horses, giving them instead the strong brotherly love that overflowed from his gentle nature.

"The only times that measly little grasshopper don't stutter's when he's chewin' the fat with one of them dumb four-legged critters, and when he lets fly one of them fists of his," a cowpuncher had once remarked, and Alex had never forgotten how the man looked as he sprawled on the ground nursing his swollen jaw.

And now Wishbone murmured disheartedly against the chestnut's neck. "Somethin' ails yuh, old timer. Tell me what it is. Why did yuh double-cross me the way yuh did yesterday? I was stakin' my last dirty shirt thet we'd win thet there race, an' now we don't even git er show ter run in the big sweepstakes nex' week. The board meets day after termorrer, an' I'll sure as hell git warned off. Poor Nanny, now she don't git ter go ter Germany, an' I promised her I'd git the jack. I gotter keep thet there promise somehow!" He sighed a shuddering sort of a sigh and urged Hell-Bent to his feet.

Carefully, with his lean, dexterous hands he went all over the gelding. "I don't git it. I jest don't git it," he muttered over and over, trying to fathom an elusive suspicion that kept just beyond his reach. "If yuh could only talk, old timer, yuh might help me. Yuh might tell me if anybody was in yuh stall, an' if so, why."

Dawn, in its dim stillness, shivered into another muggy day. It was no more chill than the zero spirits of Wishbone as he gave a last gentle pat to Hell-Bent and stretched his own aching limbs; then with lagging steps, his hands in his trousers pockets, he left the thoroughbred's stall. His head was bent forward and his eyes on the straw at his feet so that he didn't notice the skulking shadow that for a fleeting moment fell across his path. When he looked up he saw only the compassionate gaze of Alex, his expression of solemnity sitting ludicrously on his freckled visage.

Wishbone gave him a crooked, half-hearted smile and would have gone on his way but the boy stopped him with an impulsive resolute gesture.

"Gee-gosh, Wishbone, I just heard what a tumble mess you're in," he whispered, his eyes wide with fear. "Maybe—if you'd let Nanny know—she'd help, 'n' if the board seen her—they'd let you off—maybe—"

A half-startled, half-veiled expression came into the little jockey's eyes and he answered quickly as if afraid of his own thoughts, "I couldn't let Nanny know—I jest couldn't—it'd hurt her too much."

For a while they walked on in silence, crossing the old rickety bridge to Old Town and continuing along the main street of the squalid little settlement, deserted at this hour of the morning save for a few slovenly Mexicans and the Gringo hot-dog man who was just lighting the gas under his griddles. At the stand Wishbone and his companion paused. The hot-dog man greeted Alex with a cheery good-morning, but when Wishbone looked up with his usual bashful smile the hot-dog man stared through him, then flapped some hamburger and onions on the hot griddle. "Hamburg sandwich and coffee?" He addressed his remark to Alex.

"Sure, make it two," mumbled the boy, swallowing the lump that rose in his throat and giving Wishbone a quick, frightened glance; but with the exception of the red color that suddenly flamed in his smooth cheeks and the lids that dropped swiftly over his eyes, the little jockey gave no outward sign of the intended insult. But within his breast his heart felt cold and leaden. The news, then, had already spread. To those who follow the races there is no more contemptible thing than a jockey who pulls a race. A murderer even, in that wicked little border town, provokes more sympathy.

In absolute silence he forced himself to swallow the scalding coffee and gulp the hamburg sandwich, not even offering to pay for it when he had choked over the last mouthful.

Alex, painfully aware of the hurt in his friend's heart, fumbled in his own pocket and extracted the change.

In the doorway of the Turf Bar Wishbone halted. "Ah— ah—" he began and stopped, looking helplessly at Alex.

"Spill it, Wishbone, spill it," the boy encouraged.

Wishbone smiled wanly. "Ah—ah—yuh a good kid, Alex— but I know how yuh—an'—an'—them other birds feel— so—I—ah—ah—don't expect yuh ter—stick." He turned away, hunching his shoulders to push open the swinging doors.

"Gee-gosh, Wishbone, don't stand me up with them other guys! That horse's worse than a Army mule when he gets one of them cussed streaks. I know you didn't pull that race—"

Wishbone wheeled, a spark of hope lighting his eyes. "Yuh— know? How—what do yuh know?" he questioned eagerly.

"I—I don't know nothin'—exactly—exceptin' they's somethin' awful phoney about the way that hoss acted, and I know it wasn't your fault."

The lids drooped over Wishbone's eyes and his face as usual was absolutely devoid of expression. "I—got—a—idee." He gazed intently at the scuffed toes of his shoes as he spoke. "Alex, from now on yuh an' me's goin' ter change places. Ah—ah—yuh take my room—an' I'll sleep with Hell-Bent."

"Gee-gosh!" exclaimed Alex.

There was something of the old resilience in his step as Wishbone trotted swiftly back to Tia Juana. His head was up, his eyes staring straight ahead, an enigmatic smile parting his lips.

Stealthily he approached Hell-Bent's stall, but there was no need for his caution, for that part of the stable was empty. The gelding whinnied and he held out a lump of sugar. The horse munched it and rubbed his big, ugly head against the little jockey's shoulder.

"We gotter do somethin' before termorrer, old timer. We jest gotter find out somethin'," murmured Wishbone against the animal's velvet muzzle. "We jest can't git warned off. We got Nanny ter look after. Poor little Nanny—poor—Nanny." Something very like a sob caught in his throat. "Yuh the best bet I got, old timer," he went on presently. "She's dependin'—on—me. It'll jest about kill 'er—if I limp home on 'er flat tire."

The horse nosed him as if he understood and Wishbone patted him and gave him another piece of sugar.

Suddenly Hell-Bent flattened his ears and his sensitive nostrils quivered. Wishbone looked up and his eyes met those of Rivers. There was a sneer on the man's face.

"I'm quittin', see," he gibed. "I ain't workin' for no owner what hires a crooked jock!"

Not by a flicker of an eyelash did Wishbone betray the white flash of fury that seared him. "Ah—ah—who yuh trainin' fer now?" he asked quietly.

"Bennison, what owns Big Ben," snapped Rivers in some surprise.

"Look out!" suddenly warned Wishbone.

The big chestnut's hind leg shot out unexpectedly, his hoof grazing the trainer's knee. Rivers staggered back, his face ashen, "Damn brute might of killed me," he muttered.

"Too bad he didn't," said Wishbone inaudibly, stooping to pick up something that had caught his eye in the straw at his feet.

Rivers jumped toward the horse's head with upraised fist, but Wishbone straightened unexpectedly, his own head and shoulders getting in the path of the forthcoming blow. It landed with terrific force on the side of the little jockey's mouth. His eyes closed from the jarring impact and he slumped heavily against Hell-Bent.

"I knew you was crooked, but I didn't think you was a damn fool!" grunted Rivers in disgust, turning and swaggering out of the stable.

Wishbone wiped the little stream of blood that was trickling down his chin, with the back of his hand, and the smile that distorted his features would have given Rivers something to think about had he seen it.

The little jockey gazed in baffled wonder at the small piece of steel he held in his hand. "Old timer," he murmured in the gelding's ear, "I'd 'er took er lickin' any time fer yuh—an' anyways if yuh hadn't er showed yuh good hoss sense, I might er galloped all over the turf an' wasted er lot er necessary time—What the hell?"

Alex, his hair rumpled, his freckled face smeared with dirt and perspiration, stood panting before him.

"Hist!" The sound came dramatically through his teeth. He put a grimy forefinger to his lips and glanced apprehensively over his shoulder.

Wishbone slid over to him. "Wot's on yuh chest, kid?" he questioned in a sibilant whisper.

"Gee-gosh—" was all the boy could utter between gasps. He took a few gulping breaths and went on. "Do yer know the guy wot owns Big Ben?" he queried mysteriously.

Wishbone nodded his head, his face immobile. "Sh-sure—Bennison. Rivers quit ter train fer 'im."

"Yeh, but do yer know who Bennison is?"

"Can't s-say that I do." Wishbone scratched his head and then smoothed the hair with the palm of his hand where his fingers had ruffled it.

"He's the gink wot yer crowned at the Turf Bar!" stated Alex proudly.

A shadow of a smile flickered over Wishbone's lips. "I—ah—I—ah—crowned so many—I—ah—don't know wot gink yuh mean."

"The stranger, the big guy, wot tried to make yer take a drink at the Turf Bar! Gee-gosh, don't yer remember? Yer knocked him for a loop!" For a moment Alex was lost in conjured admiration, a wide grin stretching his mouth.

"Well—wot of it?" quizzed Wishbone mildly.

"Wot of it? Gee-gosh! That Bennison guy must of got the room next to yours, 'n' the walls is thin as paper. I heard 'em gassin', him 'n' Navarro—"

"How'd yuh know it was them?" interrupted Wishbone.

"Yer can't fool little Alex on that dirty Greaser's lingo, 'n' he called the big guy, Bennison. They framed yer on that race. Hell-Bent was the only hoss he was scared of, so he gets it off of Rivers that the chestnut's a ornery cuss 'n' yer the only jock wot can handle 'im, so then he tries to put yer out with doped hooch, but yer was too wise 'n' put 'em out instead. I guess yer know yer oil all right!" Alex paused to give his hero an admiring glance.

"Yeh?" Absently the little jockey was stroking the gelding's nose.

"Yeh, 'n' then they had to think of somethin' else to put yer out. They was laffin' 'n' says it worked 'n' the board was to meet tomorrer."

"Yeh?" encouraged Wishbone as Alex stopped.

"Yeh, 'n' then I runs out to spill it to yer, when out pops Navarro 'n' Bennison in the hall 'n' sees me. The big gink makes a swipe at me 'n' yells, 'Where in hell yer goin'?' I gives 'em a fast double o 'n' answers, 'I forgot to water the horses,' 'n' beats it hell-bent for election."

"Yuh-mean, Hell-bent fer Tia Juana," corrected Wishbone with his naïve smile. "N-now listen, kid," he went on, his manner changing abruptly, the smile disappearing into a set sternness about his mouth. "We gotter act an' act damn quick. Does this look familiar?" He thrust the bit of steel under the boy's astonished eyes.

"Gee-gosh—it looks like—"

"Yeh—well—n-now we gotter find the rest er wot belongs ter this here thing!"

"Gee-gosh!" said Alex.

WISHBONE DIDN'T STOP to argue. He simply stalked Rivers to his room, a dirty little hole in the wall like his own in the half-story over the dance-hall of the Turf Bar.

Wishbone sauntered through the door, his hands in his pockets, his shoulders hunched. He closed the door behind him with the same elbow and shoulder motion he used in pushing his way through swinging doors, and walked deliberately up to the astonished trainer.

Without the slightest signal, swift as a streak of lightning, his sinewy, knotted hands drove into Rivers' vulnerable spot. He crumpled like a straw in a heavy wind, the look of awe lingering on his face long after his eyes had closed.

Hastily the little jockey bent and rifled his victim's pockets. There was nothing there to warm the cold blue orbs of the jockey. He stood up and his eyes darted about the room and finally lit on a shapeless, faded, moth-eaten sweater that was thrown carelessly across the end of the bed. Into the pockets his prying fingers searched, at last closing over a broken hypodermic needle. He took the carefully wrapped steel point out of his pocket and held it beside the broken end of the needle; then he replaced the hypodermic in the sweater pocket and flung it over his arm.

Back again along the sordid main street of Old Town, its line of cheap shacks more blatantly obvious in the searching light of a gray afternoon, past a few Mexican soldiers, in their gaudy uniforms, who stared at him insolently, jockeys who turned away with an undisguised look of contempt on their usually cheerful, boyish faces, Wishbone trotted along, his hands in his pockets, a newspaper bundle tucked lovingly under his arm, his face characteristically devoid of expression, hiding well the ugly wound in his heart.

In Hell-Bent's stall he sank cross-legged on the straw, the newspaper bundle in his lap, and there waited for the veterinary whom he had summoned.

He came presently, a round little man with a shining bald head and a smooth-shaven, good-humored face and kindly gray eyes. He nodded when Wishbone rose to greet him, and went immediately to examine the horse. He went over the animal thoroughly, carefully, and paused, his fingers pressing lightly just under the left shoulder. "There's a slight swelling here. Didn't you notice it?" He inquired gently of the little jockey.

"Ah—ah—y-yes—b-but Hell-Bent often gits a shoe-boil there. He's kinder clumsy when he tries ter lie down an' doubles his feet under 'im sometimes."

"Well, this isn't any shoe-boil and I'm telling you the man that did it was a rank amateur or Hell-Bent would be a carcass by now. He jabbed the needle in the wrong place, and seems to have broken it. Hum," he mumbled on, as if to himself—"it might be a mixture of novocaine, morphine, adrenalin and strychnine, but it wasn't strong enough to do any real harm, probably only one grain of morphine."

"S-s-say, if thet there stinkin' swine'd done-in thet there hoss I'd croak 'im!" gritted Wishbone. "I—I—love Hell-Bent most as much as Nanny—an' I'd die fer her!"

The fat little veterinary sent him a veiled look of compassion, albeit his voice was brusque when he asked, "What you got in that?" He pointed to the newspaper bundle clutched in Wishbone's hand.

"Enough dope ter hang the whole layout." Gleefully he

unwrapped the parcel and held out a rumpled sweater, shape-less, faded, moth-eaten.

The veterinary took it gingerly. "Who belongs to this?" He held it at arm's length.

"L-look in the right-hand pocket."

The doctor did so and extracted a soiled and crumpled scrap of paper and the broken hypodermic needle. "Instructions from Bennison to Rivers to put a bow-legged jock, by the name of Wishbone, out good before the big sweepstakes. Hum—but where does Navarro come in?"

"Did-did-don't yuh see? Rivers failed ter bump off Hell-Bent, b-but the hoss was too sick ter race, me not guessin' it, an' so thet there lousy Spig accused me er pullin' the race. Oh—ah—ah—they slipped him some jack for it, an' Fate seemed ter—ah—sorter play right inter their dirty hands."

"Hum—well, Fate's against them this trip!"

THE SUN STRUGGLED through the dreary clouds, reminding Wishbone of his own dark troubles, that were being pushed aside to allow the great golden ball to warm and heal all humanity. The little jockey's cherubic countenance was blanker than ever as he went to the post in his gay silks.

Alex trotted along by the big chestnut's head, his steady, freckled hands on the bridle, a broad grin stretching his wide mouth. "Gee-gosh, Wishbone, ain't it a grand 'n' glorious feelin'?"

"Ah—ah—" answered Wishbone unintelligibly.

"Navarro's been showed the gate, Rivers legged it for the States 'n' Bennison's disappeared after Big Ben'd got scratched," volunteered the boy in an excited whisper, gazing worshipfully up into Wishbone's face. "Gee-gosh, we'll win easy, 'n' I don't mean maybe!"

The little jockey leaned down close to Alex. "We gotter win! I dasn't go home now—b-busted!" He spoke jerkily, trying desperately to keep his voice under control.

The boy looked up into the round expressionless eyes and thought they glistened unnaturally—and he caught his breath in a little gasp on a secret that was all his own—last night he had telegraphed Nanny.

A seething, colorful mass of humanity surged back and forth like trees swaying in the grip of a coming storm. The air was tense, heavy, still.

The post-bugle sounded; the barrier was sprung; horses lunged wildly, fighting for their heads; the jockeys hunched like flamboyant monkeys on their shoulders.

"They're off!"

Hell-Bent was away with the field, but the early speed of the others was too much for him. In the run down the back stretch he was outdistanced and trailing in last position.

Wishbone leaned suddenly back in his saddle; it had the desired effect, for the gelding shot ahead like an arrow. An eighth of a mile from the starting barrier they reached the heels of the flying pacemakers, another eighth and they were up with them, working their way warily through the field to avoid pockets and crowding. Galloping around the turn for home there was a small opening next to the rail and Wish-bone drove Hell-Bent over toward it. It was their only chance.

Now they were in the stretch and Hell-Bent was still on the rail. There were three horses tearing along in front of him, led by Lady Bug. Two other horses pounded, at their saddle-skirts.

A sea of faces loomed up before Wishbone and he could hear the frenzied cries of the throng urging them home.

Two hundred yards more and the race would be over, with Lady Bug darting along at a terrific clip, so close to the rail it seemed impossible to get Hell-Bent's massive frame through the small opening. It was too late to take the outside. No horse could make up the distance in the short run to the wire.

Wishbone glanced speculatively at Lady Bug and he thought he saw her waver slightly from the rail. To get through that tiny crevice was their only hope. Wishbone exerted every ounce of power and skill that he owned to urge Hell-Bent to the opportunity. The big chestnut gathered himself and darted through that narrow strip of daylight as straight as an arrow. As they flashed under the wire a length in front of Lady Bug, Hell-Bent's ugly, mule-like head caught the judge's eyes and it was his name that was run up in the place of honor.

Through the frantic, screaming crowd Alex struggled, clinging to the tiny hand of Nanny. Nanny, who was diminutive of stature and dainty of feature. Her white flannel sport costume clung demurely to her round, child-like figure. Her pert little periwinkle blue felt hat only half-concealed the honey-colored curls that clustered about her face, flushed like the heart of a wild rose. Her lips, of a deeper hue, were parted over small, startlingly white teeth in a happy smile. Her eyes were cornflower blue, wide open and a little stary, and she faltered slightly as she ran along beside Alex.

At sight of her Wishbone tumbled out of the saddle with an astonished yip and gathered her into his arms. "Nanny! Nanny!" he cried, great tears trickling unnoticed down his cheeks and dripping off the end of his chin. "Oh! Nanny!"

"I knew we'd win! I just knew it! Dear you! Dear Hell-Bent!" She fumbled a little and finally found the lathered neck of the racer and patted him. The big chestnut nosed her and begged for sugar. A new trainer came up with a blanket and led him back to the stables.

A short silence fell, and then Nanny said, a chiding note creeping into her low tone: "Oh, Wishbone, why didn't you tell me? Why did you leave me to worry and not know—and think maybe—maybe—you'd started to—to fight again—after you'd promised me not to?"

"Nanny! Nanny! I jest couldn't tell yuh. I was afraid yu'd count too much on winnin'—an' then if we lost—" He left his sentence unfinished to stare at the round little veterinary who sauntered up.

"It's a great world," he announced cheerfully, eyeing Nanny, who was smiling, but who seemed to be gazing in wide-eyed wonder past him. He glanced quickly over his shoulder and back again.

"Ah—ah—" began Wishbone to attract his attention. "This—ah—ah—is my little wife, Nanny. She's—blind—b-but she ain't goin' ter be after thet there eye-doctor operates, n-now that we got the jack ter go ter Germany ter see 'im." He tucked his bright silk cap in his belt and ran his fingers through his hair and then smoothed the misplaced yellow strands with the palm of his hand.

The smile suddenly faded from the lips of Nanny. "Oh, Wishbone, what'll we do with Hell-Bent? I just can't bear to leave him behind!"

"Ah—ah—" commenced Wishbone.

"Gee-gosh, Nanny," eagerly interpolated Alex, "let me keep Hell-Bent for yer."

"Hell-Bent for Tia Juana," countered Nanny, and added, a little tremor in her voice, "Isn't Wishbone the most wonderful man in the world?"

"Ah—ah—ahrrr—" mumbled Wishbone, his face flushing with embarrassment.

www.ingramcontent.com/pod-product-compliance
Lightning Source LLC
Chambersburg PA
CBHW030531020726
47494CB00004B/1306